Leaving Home

Leaving Home
Snow Globe Cafe: Book Three
Copyright © 2021 Kelly J. Calton

All rights reserved. This book or parts thereof may not be reproduced in any form, stored in any retrieval system, or transmitted in any form or by any means—electronic, mechanical, photocopy, recording, or otherwise—without prior written permission from the publisher, except as provided by United States of America copyright law.

This is a work of fiction. Names, characters, places, and incidents are either products of the author's imagination or are used fictitiously. Any resemblance to actual persons, living or dead, businesses, companies, events, or locales is entirely coincidental.

The author acknowledges the trademarked status and trademark owners of various products, bands, and/or restaurants referenced in this work of fiction, which have been used without permission. The publication/use of these trademarks is not authorized, associated with, or sponsored by the trademark owners.

ISBN-13: 978-1-7331615-2-7

KELLY J. CALTON

Leaving Home

SNOW GLOBE CAFE

BOOK THREE

With Gratitude

I'd like to dedicate this book to all my wonderful fans. You've stuck by me through some very bad times and hung in there when I wasn't well enough to make my deadlines. You all mean the world to me.

Chapter 1

EMERY COOPER LOVED DINING ALFRESCO and loved it even more when accompanied by a good friend. Sitting on a rooftop patio next to a beautiful olive tree was a far cry from the little holiday-obsessed town where she had been spending most of her time. While she loved Snow Valley and the people who lived there, it was nice being back home in San Diego.

Emery's mind was spinning with ideas to drive people to her clients' businesses in the coming months in which there were no big holiday celebrations or snow for skiing. Of course, there was the Fourth of July in a few days, but fireworks could not be a part of the celebration because of wildfires, and it kept the events to a minimum.

The small holiday-themed town had a shortage of festivities during the summer, and it was her job to teach her clients how to keep the small town hopping. Working with the city and surrounding businesses was a dream from October to May. But they would need to learn to drive business during the warmer months also.

"Earth to Emery," Lexis said, waving her fork in the air.

Emery sheepishly smiled as she realized her mind had wandered and she wasn't paying attention to her friend. Lexis was her college roommate, a pretty girl with a welcoming smile and light-green eyes. Her brunette hair with honey highlights fell in waves to her shoulders, still styled from the set of her latest movie.

This day was a gift. It was rare Lexis was off on a Friday at this time of year.

"Sorry," Emery said. "How's life on set?" Today was her last chance to catch up with Lexis as she was leaving for Snow Valley after their brunch. Unfortunately, she didn't get near enough Lexis time.

Lexis was a second-generation actor. Her mother made a splash back in the eighties first as a video vixen in rock videos, and then a few small parts in B movies. While trying to jump-start her career, she forced a twenty-year-old Lexis to go to an audition for one of those Christmas movies that were starting to get popular.

The movie needed a mother/daughter combo, and while they didn't pick her mother, they did choose a reluctant Lexis. The money was good, so she continued to make them year after year even though it wasn't her passion.

Besides, with a video vixen mother and a one-hit wonder rocker father, the only way Lexis could rebel was to become wholesome.

"Hot," Lexis said as she scrunched up her nose. "Filming a Christmas movie in LA in June is not my idea of a good time. It's so much better when we shoot in Vancouver."

Emery pushed her avocado toast around her plate.

"You know you don't have to make those movies anymore..."

Lexis sighed and shook her head. "I know, I know. Let's not go through this again. I have a plan. Save up some serious money while they'll still cast me, then get back to my artwork once I'm a has-been and have said artwork appreciated once I'm dead."

Emery laughed and shook her head. "Remember, better a has-been than a never-was," she said. "Seriously, do you have anything new? I've been starving for art since I've spent so much time in Snow Valley and haven't had time to check out your work."

Since Emery returned to San Diego she had visited some of her favorite galleries, but she was enamored with Lexis' sculptures. The girl was dripping in talent, and Emery hated the fact that she didn't use it more often.

Lexis leaned over her plate of poached eggs and looked to each side before speaking. "Unfortunately, no. This movie is sucking my soul right out of me. Devon is an absolute nightmare."

Ah, Devon. Emery had heard plenty of stories about Devon, who unfortunately had wild chemistry with Lexis on-screen, so they were cast in many movies together. He was bitter because he came to Hollywood to be a serious actor, but since he'd gotten himself in debt from low-paying server gigs and high rent prices, he took the parts in the quaint, charming holiday movies. He hated every second of it.

"I'm sorry," Emery said sincerely. "I know you hate working with him."

"I only have one more month," Lexis said. "I'm taking a few for myself after that. You're right. I need to get back to my art. What about you? How long are you planning on being in Snow Valley this time?"

Emery smiled and thanked the good-looking waiter as he refilled her mimosa. He gave her a flirtatious wink as he walked away.

"Since I'm technically homeless, who knows?" she said.

Receiving an offer she couldn't refuse from the next-door neighbor in her condominium complex, Emery sold her first home. By the time brunch was finished, the movers would have most of her possessions in storage and the rest on a truck to Snow Valley, including her car.

"I need to finish up my work there," Emery said. She owned a side business as a social media marketing coach, and her protégés in the small town were all very close to graduating from her tutelage.

Sugar Jones was her business partner and very best friend in the world since the second grade. She was an incredibly talented pastry chef, and the two of them had turned the cupcake stand they started at twelve years old into a thriving company and substantial online presence.

At twenty-six, Emery Cooper appeared to have it all. Not only was she the co-CEO of Sugar Jones, LLC, but she also built her own business helping other professionals manage their online presence and marketing. Sugar's new hometown was currently her biggest client.

The chamber of commerce hired her to help build the town up and keep the tourists coming year round. Per Emery's recommendation, they now had a full-blown social media manager, and Emery's time working with them was coming to an end. Once the summer was over, the town should be able to market itself effectively.

They would have plenty of momentum to build on by fall, and it was easy to keep things going in the winter with all the holidays and cold-weather activities. Moreover, Sugar's father owned a major attraction—a large resort called The Lodge, which also contained private, luxury log cabins on the property. The rich and famous flocked to the grandiose cabins when they craved privacy for their family and friends, and the grand lodge, with over two hundred and forty rooms suitable for the upper-middle class, were booked all fall and winter.

"You better not end up moving there," Lexis said as she wrinkled her nose. "That town is way too much like one of my movie sets. I could barely bring myself to go for Sugar's wedding."

Luckily, Lexis and Sugar became thick as thieves on their first meeting back in the day, so Emery was blessed to have this incredible circle. Lexis even stood up at Sugar's wedding, with Emery being the maid of honor.

Emery laughed as she took a sip of her mimosa. "Not likely," she said as Lexis squinted her eyes. "Seriously, California is my home."

"Okay, if you say so," Lexis said. "It's not like you would want to live by Sugar and Becca or—what was his name? Oh yes, Alec. Hell, I'd move there for Alec." Lexis wiggled her eyebrows.

"You're too funny," Emery said as she piled her silverware and napkin on her plate. "I told you, Alec is just a client and Sugar's brother. A thing between us is never going to happen."

Lexis threw her head back with a hearty laugh. "Have

you watched any of my movies? Saying something like that is bound to make it happen. Have you learned nothing from me?"

Emery slid her card into the receipt book and handed it to the waiter. "Yeah, I learned how to be a real pain in the—"

Her ringing cell phone stopped her mid-sentence as the name Alec with his picture popped up on her screen.

"Nothing. You've learned nothing," Lexis said, shaking her head.

☙

Emery closed her laptop and took in the gorgeous scenery around her. She was surprised by the excitement fluttering in her stomach as the train flowed through the mountains, curving along the mountainside. Colorful wildflowers danced in the lush shades of green.

The last time she was here was for Sugar's small, intimate wedding this spring. She married Jackson Anderson after a whirlwind romance, and Emery would expect nothing less. Snow covered the ground in April, which boggled Emery's mind. In the spring, trying to plan anything for this town seemed futile since most people were over the winter weather, so she was diving into summer headfirst.

Emery needed to figure out how to drive people to the town even if there wasn't snow or a major holiday. Even though she was about to set the town free to manage their own social media, she felt she needed to stick with it through this summer because of the level of difficulty.

Emery rested her chin in her hand and gazed happily

out the window. Her first trip on this train scared the life out of her. The train hugged the side of the mountain as it wound around its glorious curves. It made for a breathtaking sight, but the drop-down was terrifying at first view. However, she'd ridden this train enough now that the wonder of the landscape drowned out her fears.

While she had conquered her fear of the train, driving on the side of the mountain still terrified her. She grew up in nearly perfect weather in San Diego, and the mountains by the coast were hills compared to the Rockies. She didn't know if she'd ever be comfortable driving to Snow Valley, especially when only a little rickety wooden fence was between you and a sharp drop off.

Alec, her best friend, Sugar's, half-brother, had offered to meet her in California and take over the mountain driving, but Emery decided it was best to fly in and then take the train. He was considerate, and that was the reason for his call earlier during her brunch—to be sure everything was on schedule. Emery had already made plans to have her vehicle delivered to Snow Valley, so she didn't see any reason to change those plans.

If she were honest with herself, being in a vehicle with Alec that long didn't seem like the best idea. He was handsome, with clear, light-blue eyes and a mouth that was too pretty to be on a man. The sharp, Nordic jawline and cheekbones balanced the pretty, and he wore his dirty-blond hair just a tad too long, with it curling along the top of his collar.

Charm dripped off the man like honey—warm, rich, and inviting. With a lazy smile and a quick wit, Alec Larsson could have about any woman he wanted. Emery had the feeling that he did . . . frequently. The fact that he was honest might explain the lack of embittered females. Alec was all about fun and good times and, from what Emery had heard, made sure any of his dalliances were well aware of this fact.

Still, you couldn't help but like the man. Even though he drove her absolutely nuts with his penchant for missing deadlines, she still enjoyed working with him. His crazy energy always made things fun and interesting. Alec co-owned a new endeavor on The Lodge's property, and the marketing for it was Emery's pet project.

People who valued experiences more than luxury coveted a hotel like Snow Valley Hotel. The rooms there were clean and basic. People staying at the hotel didn't want to be in their rooms unless they were sleeping.

There was an attraction between Emery and Alec for sure, but she would never cross that line. Sure, she always felt invigorated while she was around him. He pushed her out of her comfort zone of organization and deadlines, and she always laughed and had a good time while working with him.

The fact that he was her best friend's brother made him strictly off-limits in Emery's mind. Sugar, her daughter, Violet, and Sugar's mother, Becca, were her family. If they started something and it ended ugly, things would never be the same for any of them.

Emery loved her biological family and was in the process of coming to terms with the fact that they were just different. Her siblings had gone off to college before she finished grade school. And as most high schoolers would, they viewed Emery as an annoyance, someone they had to watch after school instead of hanging out with their friends.

Since her parents had high-powered, stressful jobs, her siblings watched Emery a lot. Her parents, Laura and Avery, were the ultimate power couple. Laura was a successful literary agent, and Avery was an entertainment lawyer. They both housed big names as clients and swam the entertainment business's shark-infested waters like two great whites in perfect sync.

She smiled as she thought about meeting Sugar in the second grade. They became fast friends, and Emery's parents took on Becca as a client. Beatrice the Butterfly, a character Becca created to help children with complex issues like bullying, was a smash hit and made all their careers.

Emery spent a good amount of time with Becca and Sugar, which showed her a different side to parenting. She loved her parents with all her heart, but Becca's kind, warm, maternal parenting was soothing and comforting. Emery liked to think she grew up with the best of both worlds—parents who valued achievement and drive, and an old-fashioned surrogate mom who baked cookies and read stories at bedtime.

Her chest filled with excitement as the small town of Snow Valley came into view. This was her favorite part of the train ride as she could look down on the valley and see the beautiful town laid before her. The big square was the most visible, with tall buildings housing shops and apartments surrounding it on all four sides.

This was the center of it all, with smaller houses dotting the landscape, spiraling outward from the square. To the north of it she could make out The Lodge between the tall evergreens and what she knew was a few miles away, the Snow Valley Hotel. In the winter, if she strained her eyes enough she could see the skiers taking a run down The Lodge's many slopes.

Emery took this town in like her very own newborn baby, and now they were ready to walk all on their own. While Emery was a business person through and through, she also took the town on as a client because she knew the publicity they would receive from Sugar's appearance on *The Holiday Baking Extravaganza* last Christmas.

In the trenches since she was a teenager, Emery knew how to win the battle with social media. Along with Sugar and her daughter, Violet, Emery owned Sugar Jones, LLC, or SJL. They were just a mere fifteen years old when a unicorn cupcake made them internet famous.

With Sugar's artistic talent, Emery's natural-born skills for business and marketing, and Josh—may he rest in peace—the computer genius, they took their opportunity and ran. Over the years, millions upon millions had visited their social media pages and website. A paid sponsorship in one of their YouTube videos costs in the mid-five figures.

With all this knowledge, Emery wanted to help the little guy. Sugar's family may be the big fish in this small town, but many small businesses could be buffed up to shine like a new penny with the proper marketing and social media presence. SJL was about to shine a light on their little town, and Emery was there to make sure they were ready.

And ready they were. Emery was coming to town to wrap up a few loose ends with her pupils, and they would be prepared to fly on their own. Sure, Sugar's Snow Globe Café brought in a lot of business, but the town's small business owners had embraced social media and were now masters of their destiny.

They also embraced Emery with open arms, and she was genuinely smitten with the good people of Snow Valley. But, deep down, if she were honest, she was a little worried at first about being accepted. A town founded by people of Norwegian ancestry was short on diversity.

Emery was a melting pot of diversity. Her father would be a perfect fit for a town like this. Tall, blond, and green-eyed, Avery Cooper would blend right in. Her mom, Laura, was half Mexican and half African American and would stand out on the streets of Snow Valley.

Together these two made Emery, who could be just about any nationality she wanted. Her mocha skin could be Mexican, African American, Italian, or Caucasian with a good tan. But how she was perceived depended a lot on how she wore her hair. It was curly, but she could blow it out straight or wear it in waves. Her large hazel-green eyes were her favorite feature, and her whole life, she was constantly asked, "What are you?"

If Sugar were in hearing distance, she would always snap back with, "She's human. What the hell are you?" But Emery would smile and answer the question, no matter how old it got. So yes, she faced her fair share of people not accepting her. So far, the people of Snow Valley were terrific, but she's experienced the accepting type turn heel on her before.

She truly hoped these people were not like that because she felt a kinship with a lot of the small business owners of Snow Valley.

Sliding her laptop into its case, Emery rested her head against the cool glass as the train made the descent to Snow Valley. She couldn't wait to see Sugar, Becca, and Violet again, and maybe, just maybe, a tiny part of her excitement was because Alec was picking her up from the train station.

Alec Larsson leaned lazily on the front of his truck, his long legs and arms crossed. He looked up at the perfect crystal-clear blue sky and sighed. Big puffy clouds drifted by, and Alec smiled, thinking about how his niece and sister would try to make animals out of them. Even though he'd only known them a short while, they'd both become so essential to him.

It was all so complicated but so worth it. Alec's father didn't know about his sister Sugar until last fall. Becca, Eric's new stepmother, had kept her a secret. Alec knew it had something to do with his grandfather, and he had a feeling he didn't know half of it. From what he knew of Becca, she must have had good reason. You couldn't help but love her—she was so kind and gentle. Becca wouldn't do something purely for spite or because she was bitter.

Sugar was younger than the twins, so there was no denying that Eric cheated on his wife. Of course, a situation like this would generally send shock waves through a family when revealed, but considering his mother and father were in a sham of a marriage because of his grandfather, it wasn't as harmful as one might imagine.

There was so much to process when everything went down last fall, and he didn't have time to question his father.

It was clear that his father, Eric, and Becca were meant for each other. This was not some case of meeting again during your second act in life and reigniting a spark. If there was such a thing as soul mates, Eric and Becca were the poster children.

The only logical conclusion was that his grandfather must have threatened to write Eric out of the business and the wealth that accompanied it, but logic didn't have a place in scenario. He didn't think his father cared a rat's ass about any of that. Yes, he knew Eric loved The Lodge, but Alec knew he loved Becca more.

John Larsson died in a fiery crash with Alec's maternal grandfather. Alec was fifteen years old at the time, and the ink on their death certificates hadn't dried before his parents were signing their divorce papers. His mother came out as a lesbian, and his parents remained great friends.

The man was an enigma, and he doted on Alec. One thing for sure, his grandfather was one scary dude. It made Alec uneasy to think that perhaps his grandfather did something sinister to keep Becca away, but deep down, it wouldn't surprise him. Keeping The Lodge in the Larsson family was paramount to his grandfather, so uniting two founding families would warrant extreme action.

"Good morning, Alec!" Mrs. Svetlana called cheerily as she power walked her way down the sidewalk, pumping her arms to the beat of the music playing in her earbuds.

"Good morning, Mrs. Svetlana," Alec called back with a broad smile and a wave. Such was the life of living in a small town—everyone knew everyone. But for Alec and his family, it was more than that because they employed over half the town. Mrs. Svetlana had worked at The Lodge for nearly twenty years.

Being the heir apparent to the family business could

be a real thorn in Alec's side. Growing up, he could do no wrong in anyone's eyes. He could probably knock over a bank right now, and people would shake their heads and say, "Oh, that Alec, he's so precocious."

It was infuriating. Alec hadn't realized how much special treatment he received until he went away from here and off to college. Being at a big university on the east coast opened his eyes to how privileged he was. While most might revel in that type of environment, Alec found it stifling and wondered if he could ever make a mark as his own man.

Take his photography, for example. For most of Alec's young life, all he wanted to do was take pictures. His paternal grandparents hated it since they expected Alec to take over operations at The Lodge. His mother and father nurtured his talent and supported him one hundred percent.

Then came the misunderstanding that caused him to rethink exactly how talented he was. Perhaps people just told him that because of who he was and what he could do for them. However, by the time he knew the truth, Alec had made up his mind—he would devote himself to the family business and treat his first love as a hobby.

Pushing the dark thoughts away, he looked at his phone. The train should be pulling up any minute now. Alec tried to squash the excitement that was bubbling up in his stomach at the thought of Emery being back in town. His sister's best friend and business partner was off-limits for any kind of romantic relationship.

One thing he could definitively say about Emery was that she didn't extend any special treatment to him. Alec had never met anyone like her before. Not only did she not view him as the crowned prince of a vast empire, but he also got the feeling he annoyed her.

Alec couldn't help but smile at the thought of how her extremely well-maintained façade would almost erupt into anger when he didn't turn an assignment in on time. But instead, he found himself turning things in late on purpose to get a rise out of her.

Emery spent the last eight months bringing his family business kicking and screaming into the world of social media marketing. He couldn't deny the results, but Alec was a much more unplugged type of guy. Since his offshoot hotel didn't have a big budget yet, Alec and his partner, Jackson, provided Emery with content for their social media accounts.

The task fit Alec like a glove. Sending in pictures and videos displaying the beauty of nature and the hotel's fun activities hardly counted as work for Alec. And despite his enthusiasm for sharing the content with Emery, he knew that he if he sent it a little, she would come looking for him.

Emery was a talented and organized professional, but it didn't hurt that she was also beautiful. Reaching five foot ten with a slim physique, she was a head turner. Her face was all big hazel eyes with luscious lips, and her skin was the perfect shade of mocha. Her blended ancestry came together to make a perfect woman in Alec's eyes. She frequently wore her long, curly dark-brunette hair in a high ponytail, and on more than one occasion, Alec found himself wanting to yank that hair tie out and run his hands through her hair.

His phone vibrated in his pocket, and he saw a text from Emery. Ever efficient, she was letting him know the train would be pulling up in five minutes. Squashing the sudden fluttering in his stomach, he took the stairs leading to the train platform two at a time.

He couldn't help but wonder if she was considering making a permanent move to Snow Valley. Emery fit in this town like a glove. But if he were honest with himself, he almost wished she'd fail her current mission. This town was slam-packed with visitors from Halloween until spring, with their perfect ski slopes and holiday-themed events.

It was nice to have a small break in the summer to recoup and relax. Sure, it seemed like Alec breezed through this perfect world, but he worked many hard hours. He was just lucky that it was doing something he loved, even if it was not his first passion.

Madison, his twin sister, ended that dream, and he would never forgive her. Alec's brows knitted to a tight *V* shape as he thought about how his sister and Emery grew closer and closer to Madison. They had experienced some of her shenanigans but decided she was worth a second try. He just hoped their trust didn't lead to drama and hurt feelings.

The train pulled into the station as Alec hit the platform, his excitement at seeing Emery again chasing away memories of failed dreams and betrayal.

○≺

Emery watched the lovely scenery as Alec drove toward the Snow Globe Café. After getting married, Sugar had vacated the apartment above the quaint café, so Emery would stay there while working in town. Unfortunately, even though Sugar loved living above the bakery, three cats, a rather large dog, a relatively small child, and a six-foot-five inches tall husband proved to be too much for the small apartment.

"I don't know why you don't stay in one of the cabins," Alex said as he turned in the direction of the town square instead of The Lodge property. "We all live there now."

Sugar and her growing family moved in one of those "spare" cabins. The Lodge had several where relatives used to live or for when they came to visit.

"This is more practical," Emery pointed out. "Most of my work will involve the square, so I want to be close to it. Besides, we also have the new property to deal with."

SJL had purchased a building in Snow Valley. Sugar inherited the Snow Globe Café, and two buildings to her left decided they wanted to sell. The owners were older and decided it was time to retire. The café was standing room only, so expanding it was practical. Sugar purchased the one directly next to the café, and their business bought the one next to that.

They bought the second building as an investment property. For now, there were two occupied apartments above the storefront, just like Sugar's café. The street level had been a novelty shop that offered Snow Valley and Colorado merchandise.

"Have you decided what you're going to do with the extra property?" Alec asked.

Emery took a deep breath of fresh mountain air as dazzling views of towering pines sped by her window. "Not yet. Sugar has some ideas but insists on talking about it in person."

Alec chuckled, taking his eyes from the road

momentarily to smile at Emery. He was incredibly handsome, especially when he smiled. In board shorts and a nice fitting T-shirt, Alec would easily fit in with the surfers in Emery's native California.

"What?" Emery asked.

"You know what," Alec said. "If I know my sister, she has some plan up her sleeve to keep you here."

Emery sighed. In her heart, she knew Alec was right. Sugar had a one-track mind when she wanted something, and what she wanted now more than anything in the world was for Emery to move to Snow Valley.

Just as she was about to answer, a deer darted out into the road. Emery was too terrified to scream as Alec slammed on the brakes, sending the truck sideways. His arm flew across Emery, his hand clasping her right shoulder as he tried to regain control of the large vehicle.

Emery saw the view of the outside world swirl while she clutched Alec's arm. The truck finally came to a stop facing the wrong direction and almost landing in the ditch. Her pulse raced as she drew in a deep breath. Still in the middle of the road, the deer looked at them, and unimpressed, sauntered into the woods.

"Emery, are you okay?" Alec asked with concern.

He undid his seatbelt and gently cupped Emery's face when she didn't answer. "Em, are you all right?"

Her gaze fell right into the depths of his light-blue eyes, her heart skipping a beat when she saw the care and concern which seemed to be staring straight into her very soul.

Emery squeezed her eyes shut tight and tried to orient her thoughts. "You didn't turn in next week's schedule first thing this morning as we planned," Emery blurted out. She had taken a vow not to bring it up since he seemed to get a kick out of riling her up, but it was just the first thing that came to her mind. And it felt like the only safe subject after such a tense moment between them.

A monstrous grin that would leave even the strongest of women feeling faint spread across Alec's handsome face. His thumb gently stroked her cheek as he looked at her tenderly. "Yeah, you're okay," he said softly.

She could not explain how she felt in that moment. It was somewhere between relieved, vulnerable, and terrified. Emery felt her heart opening to Alec, and that was simply not supposed to happen. One unguarded moment and he seemed to slip right in.

A loud honk broke the couple from their thoughts as Alec reluctantly turned his attention back to the road. He expertly turned the vehicle around, heading back in the right direction.

"I'm so sorry, Em, really I am," Alec said as his eyes stayed focused on the road. "I was speeding and wasn't paying close enough attention to the road."

Compassion spread through Emery as she experienced this many times with her best friend and Alec's sister. Sugar suffered from severe ADHD as a child, and knowing what she knows, it wouldn't surprise her to learn that Alec had some form of it. Between his driving habits and his inability to do anything on time, he showed classic symptoms.

"It wasn't your fault," Emery said firmly but softly. "That could have happened to anyone. It's the deer's fault. You should have seen the way it looked at us before it hopped back in the forest like we were wasting its time."

Alec chuckled, and Emery tried to relax again. Anything close to a car accident was a trigger for her and a an even bigger trigger for Sugar.

"We might not want to mention this to Sugar," Emery added, thinking about her friend. Sugar's first husband and Emery's other best friend had died in a car crash.

Alec told a fantastic story, and Emery could picture the tale he would tell, embellished, of course. Their car would be hanging off the mountain before he was done, and that would put Sugar in hysterics.

"Oh, I didn't even think of that," Alec said as he came to the main stoplight leading into town. Then, as the truck rolled to a stop at the red light, he looked over at Emery.

"You sure you're okay?" he asked tenderly as he gave her hand a quick squeeze. "Josh was important to you too."

Before she could think about it, a baseball-sized lump formed in her throat. She took a deep breath and swallowed it down. She usually took care of people, not the other way around, and the care and sincerity in his voice just smashed right into Emery's chest.

"I'm fine," she said and gave Alec a dazzling smile. She knew it was her best asset and was grateful that her second-best asset, her big hazel-green eyes, were hidden behind oversized sunglasses. Eyes welling up with tears would be a dead giveaway that she wasn't okay, and she just needed to hold her eyes open without blinking a few more seconds, and those tears wouldn't make it out of her eyes alive.

"Seriously, Alec, I'm all right," Emery said. Alec looked at her quizzically, and when the light turned green, he still sat there, staring at her like it was the first time they'd ever met. Then, finally, a horn blared behind them, and Alec cleared his throat, turned his face back to the road, and drove.

"Do you want me to drop you off at the café apartment?" Alec asked as he turned down the road that led to the big town square.

"No, the new building would be fine," Emery said, peering out the window to get a good look. "I talked to Sugar on the train, and she's shooting today. She said I could go to the new place first as long as I don't go upstairs."

When they arrived, Alec looked disappointed to find only one small bag containing Emery's essentials and her laptop. He had carried many a bag up the stairs leading to the apartments above the Snow Globe Café.

"You know, I was expecting to get my cardio today. Now I'm going to have to go climbing or something this afternoon," he kidded.

"I packed everything in boxes for the movers to save your back this time," Emery chuckled. Now that she looked back, it was always Alec who helped her when she came into town.

He pulled the truck into the alley behind the square and put the vehicle in park. "I appreciate that," he said with mock seriousness. "You sure you don't need any help?"

"I'm good," Emery said. "Thanks again for picking me up. You poor thing, you always seem to get stuck giving me a ride."

"Pleasure's mine," Alex said with a smile as Emery exited the vehicle. "I'm just always happy to see you've come back."

Emery couldn't help the wide smile that erupted over her face at his charming words. Then, with a final wave, she left to see their new property.

Chapter 2

EMERY LOOKED OVER THE TOWN SQUARE as people bustled by her on the sidewalk. This town was so lovely. Designed like old European towns, it had an enormous square dead center in the middle where all the towns' activities took place. Surrounding the square on all four sides were tall, shiny gray stone buildings containing large storybook windows. The square was a riot of color with flowers growing everywhere.

The town made you feel like you were in a different time—when people knew their neighbors. When things were just a little slower, people didn't worry about likes or how they looked on social media. It was a breath of fresh air in a world that could be so repugnant.

Still, the town did need a few improvements, and Snow Valley had taken up most of her time since she and Sugar had followed an unknowing Becca last year. Emery became the town's social media mentor and did what she could to bring more attention to this little piece of heaven on earth.

She smiled as she saw the stand that contained a big screen on one side of the square. The chamber of commerce listened to her and made their normal once-a-year viewing of *The Rocky Horror Picture Show* a movie night every weekend during the summer, with the town's residents voting on what movie to play each Saturday night.

They also had several selfie stations strategically placed along the square. Emery had recommended an artist friend of hers, and he did a beautiful job. Her heart warmed when she noticed a family taking turns to be a butterfly, taking pictures and making memories.

Alec's twin, Madison, informed Emery that many of the guests in their central hotel were venturing into the square for movie nights, farmers market, and other activities. It seemed that wholesome entertainment fit their guests well, and the people of Snow Valley were reaping the rewards.

Entering their new property, Emery looked around the cavernous room with a critical eye. Like most things in this town, the previous owners had taken pride in their shop, and it was in great shape. They wanted to retire, and since their children moved away and weren't interested in continuing the family business, they were left with no other choice but to sell. Emery hoped whoever opened shop here would put in the same amount of care the previous owners had for their business.

Most of the shelves and racks from when it was a novelty shop had been moved out, leaving an enormous empty room. The goodies found here were fine, but customers could find T-shirts and the like in the actual square. Emery hoped whoever rented this place from SJL would do something different that drove traffic to the square.

The front of the store had massive windows giving the shoppers who walked down the bustling square a great view of whatever treasures were inside. All the shops around the square had prime real estate to draw customers, and this building was on the end with windows on the side as well. Light poured in, giving it all so much potential.

The front door flew open, and in came the tornado of energy that was her best friend, Sugar Jones. Dressed in her ever-present yoga pants, she had her pink chef's coat open, revealing a white tank top. Sugar swept up her long, blonde hair in a bun, and she nearly knocked Emery off her feet with a gigantic hug.

"Sweet baby Jesus, I missed you," Sugar said as she hung onto her best friend.

Emery laughed as she hugged her back. "I missed you too."

"Three months is entirely too long for you to be gone, " Sugar said as she let go of her friend.

"I know, but may I point out that you are the one that moved away, not me," Emery said. Sure, they FaceTimed every day—well, several times a day. But SJL also had Zoom meetings at least a couple of times a week where they were both involved.

"Just a technicality," Sugar said. "You haven't gone upstairs, right?"

"No, I haven't, just like I promised."

When their business bought the building, it was discovered that the tenant in one of the spacious apartments upstairs had destroyed it. Everything needed to be repaired or replaced. As a team, Sugar and Emery decided to make an official office for SJL.

The company's employees had always worked from home. From the bakers making videos to the editors who turned them into sleek, professional videos to the IT team that kept it all running, they all worked from home. Of course, SJL employees would still have that option, but some could work from an office now if wanted, and now they had the ease of team retreats or quarterly meetings where they could all come together.

They headed to the back alley to climb the stairs to the office. As they reached the top, Sugar grabbed the railing, faltering a bit.

"Whoa," she said as she gathered her bearings.

Emery grabbed her arm and helped her enter the office. "Are you okay?"

"Yeah, I'm fine," Sugar reassured her. "I don't think I've eaten today. Things were crazy with the shoot."

Their brand had expanded to full-length baking shows on YouTube, with TikTok teasers. Emery worried about Sugar burning the candle at both ends, which was one of the reasons they came to a significant decision.

They were both taking a step back from the business. SJL had consumed them since they were kids. Sometimes Emery will see a fifteen-year-old out and about and wonder how the heck they managed what they did at that age.

Luckily, they had parents to guide them properly when they went viral all those years ago. Of course, it didn't hurt that Josh, their dearly departed partner, was a computer genius. It also didn't hurt that he would do anything to spend more time with Sugar at that time.

Emery was proud of what they had achieved over the last decade. Neither of them let the success go to their heads and they'd been responsible with the bounty they received over the years. Living frugally and saving left them both in a position of great freedom.

When Sugar married Jackson Anderson in the early spring of this year, Emery couldn't have been happier for her best friend. But she also realized things would need to change. Of course, they would always be best friends, but Sugar needed to spend time with her new husband and adjust to their family dynamic, whether she knew it or not. Jackson adopted Sugar's daughter, Violet, so they needed to get their footing as a family.

If Sugar had her way, she would have built a back bedroom for Emery. But deep down, Emery knew she should stay out of the picture, even for just a little bit, to give them all a chance to learn their new normal. They stayed in touch every day not only because of their friendship but because of their thriving company.

Back when Sugar married Josh, the three of them were a complete unit. Even though Emery knew there were many problems at play with Josh's alcohol addiction, she also knew they never had the chance to be a normal married couple because of her constant presence in their life.

She wasn't naïve enough to think the outcome would have been different if she weren't in the picture, but somewhere in the back of her mind, Emery wondered a bit because she was human after all.

Still, Sugar needed to have her family separate from her. Yes, she would always be Sugar's sister. However, typical sisters weren't as involved in each other's lives, and deep down Emery knew this needed to happen.

Uprooting herself to follow Sugar here seemed like the wrong thing to do at the time. Now that Sugar's family had set up roots it wouldn't be entirely out of the picture for her to live here. The thing is if Emery ended up in Snow Valley, she needed her reasons and purpose for being there, not just to live near Sugar and Violet.

Stepping back from SJL and hiring out their parts in the company were all part of that. They were lucky and already had amazing bakers on staff to create cute videos. In addition, local video editors were hired who would also produce Sugar's monthly baking show.

The partners both agreed to promote Emery's right hand, Vanessa. She had worked for SJL almost from the very beginning and was a big part of why they were a huge success. A foster child most of her life, she started working at SJL when she was barely out of high school and worked her way through college.

Vanessa would slide right into the position of President, and she would be moving to Snow Valley. She'd been a city kid most of her life, but Vanessa had a son the same age as Violet and bringing him up in this small town appealed to her greatly. Once Emery assured her how good the schools were and how low the crime was, she started packing.

They also hired someone to replace Vanessa, and the new employee had been training remotely with her for a couple of weeks. Local to Snow Valley, she would be coming into the office.

Emery would be lying if she said she wasn't scared. This business was so ingrained in her life, it felt like giving up part of her identity. On the other hand, it was exciting, thinking about the possibilities with the free time she would now have. Her only work with the business would be a weekly meeting with Vanessa to make sure everything was functioning as it should.

Sugar's only participation would be her monthly baking videos. They had plenty of short-form content built up, even if they hadn't had bakers on staff. She may do a little promotion here and there for the brand, but other than that, she was going to be pretty hands-off.

Stepping into the space above the shop, Emery didn't find an apartment but a comfortable, aesthetically pleasing office space. This was not a quaint apartment like the French country-style apartment above the café, but it was laid out similarly.

They entered the kitchen area, but unlike the full-service kitchen in Sugar's apartment, this one only had a microwave and a refrigerator.

The contractors had removed the stove and peninsula separating the small dining area from the kitchen. Only one counter and the sink had survived. The counter had an electric kettle and what happened to be Emery's favorite coffee machine. A glass table that seated six was in the middle of what was the old kitchen. Along the wall perpendicular to the counter were a couple of comfortable but elegant mint green chairs separated by a table.

On the table was a picture of Joshua Jones, their original partner and best friend. Emery picked up the picture and smiled at the then eighteen-year-old boy. His high school graduation robe was open with a t-shirt showing that said 'When all else fails ctrl alt delete'.

She lovingly ran her hand down the smooth frame. This is the Josh she chose to remember. The Josh before college. The Josh before the drinking. The Josh who just loved this girl Sugar and was best friends with a girl named Emery.

"He needed to be here," Sugar said quietly as Emery put the picture back on the table. "I thought this picture would be how he'd like to be remembered."

Emery smiled at her friend. "I think so too. He'd also love it that you put him close to the food." Both friends laughed and continued the tour.

The living room contained a large conference table with a big screen hung over the impressive brick fireplace. The colors of this office space were the same as the SJL logo—mint green, peach, lavender, and pink. The walls were mostly a light peach, and accents around the apartment contained the other colors.

Two more cubicles were on the wall next to the fireplace. Two more new employees from Snow Valley would be filling those desks. One was financial, and one was for social media.

Looking to her right, the contractors had removed the door and opened up the entryway. Cubicle partitions were in place to separate it into different offices. The second bedroom still had a door with a silver nameplate that read "Vanessa Hughes, President." Outside the door was a glass T-shaped desk with a monitor.

"I'm impressed," Emery said. This had all been done in such a short amount of time and was exactly the way she wanted. Considering she was conferenced in over the phone for much of the planning, it pleased her that her vision had come to fruition.

"I know, right?" Sugar said as she walked into Vanessa's new office. "Vanessa's going to be in town in a couple of weeks. We should get her some plants or something."

"I have some business on the square tomorrow. I'll check out Holly's place. I haven't had a chance to say hello to her since I got back in town anyway," Emery said. Holly owned a local floral shop and had become a dear friend to both Sugar and Emery.

This apartment had a third bedroom, as this building was more significant than the café or its neighbor that made the café extension a reality. This room housed an office for Emery and Sugar. So even though they were taking a step back from the company, they would always have a presence. Two twin, L-shaped desks took up most of the room.

Emery ran her hand over the smooth glass top and smiled when she noticed an organizer filled with office supplies. Post-its, paper clips, a stapler, and random highlighters and pens filled the black cavities. If she was going to be bribed to stay somewhere, organizational office supplies were a strong motivator.

"We are doing the right thing, right?" Sugar asked quietly as she sat on her desk. "Everything, and I mean everything, in our lives has changed in the last nine months. Should we be doing another big change right now?"

Emery sighed. "I'd be lying if I said I wasn't just a little frightened by all this," she said. "It's time, though, Sug. All the changes are why we need to do this. We need to find our new normal. We've been on autopilot doing this for years. Not many people are lucky enough to have a choice, and since we do, I think it's important we grab it."

As she said the words, Emery's fear began to lessen and her resolve strengthened. It had been a long time since she felt excited about the SJL business. Truth be told, it was never her dream, and she just realized she was a complete hypocrite when she was lecturing her friend Lexi about doing Christmas movies when her passion laid elsewhere. But, yes, this was the right thing to do.

If she were honest with herself, Emery hadn't thought about what she wanted to be since she was a pre-teen. But then things happened so fast for them, she didn't have time to think about what she wanted. Sugar always knew she wanted to be a baker, but Emery didn't have the luxury of that kind of certainty when she was a child.

Emery and Sugar had sold cupcakes and cookies at a local farmers market in San Diego when they were thirteen. Their friend Josh tagged along to help, but really he tagged along because of his massive crush on Sugar.

The friends sold out every week. No matter how much product Sugar created, they were selling out. Sugar began doing more intricate designs as her talents improved, and Emery took a video with her phone of Sugar making a cupcake with frosting piped to resemble a unicorn.

After Josh played with the speed, making the twenty-minute video into three minutes, he uploaded it to YouTube. Becca, Sugar's mom, allowed them to do so as long as Sugar's face wasn't in the videos. As a result, they inadvertently stumbled upon a new trend, and they blew up.

Emery didn't know the exact number of their reach, but it was well into the tens of millions at this point. The fact that she didn't know the precise number caused her to pause, as it used to be the first thing she looked at every day—their social numbers. It had been so exciting for so long.

Emery enjoyed the challenge of running a big social media company. She enjoyed the climbing numbers and figuring out how to drive traffic and followers to their social media accounts. Now SJL was a juggernaut in the social media world and the challenge just wasn't there anymore.

These last few years, the business started losing its appeal. In the grand scheme of it all, what did having a large social following really mean, besides great business? Emery had given her all to SJL and didn't let something like what she wanted to do when she was a little girl figure into things.

Back then, they had hit the lottery. It could have been a one-time deal, but the three friends worked incredibly hard to sustain their success. Any dreams before that were tossed to the side, and Emery turned out to be very good at marketing and running a growing business.

Now Sugar could concentrate on her bakery, and Emery could do what she wanted to do. It was exciting to think that she had no idea what that was, which was entirely out of character for her.

Sugar pushed herself off the desk. "Come on, let's go check out the space downstairs. Jackson should be bringing Violet by in a little bit."

They walked back down the stairs and into the large retail area on the ground level. This building was larger because of its corner location, and it was cavernous. At the back was ample space for inventory and a few offices.

"Wow," Emery said with a bit of an echo to her voice. "This place is huge. It could be anything."

Sugar was over by the side windows and was holding what looked to be a painting.

"I know," Sugar said distractedly. "That's what worries me."

"What's that?" Emery asked as she walked over to her friend.

"They must have forgotten this picture," Sugar said as she handed it over to her friend.

"This is amazing." Emery looked at the large photograph with a critical eye. It was gorgeous. The photographer shot it from very high, so whoever did it must have climbed one of the higher mountains in the area. The shot contained The Lodge and the square. Alec and Jackson's new hotel wasn't in the picture, so it was older. This couldn't have been a drone.

It was majestic in scope, and the composition was perfect. It took Emery's breath away. Of course, most people can take a decent picture with how good cell phone cameras are, but this photograph was art.

Taking the picture, she flipped it over to see if there was a signature. Disappointment settled in when she found it blank. She would love to see more of this person's art.

"We'll have to contact the Farrows. I'm sure they'd want this back," Emery said as she handed the picture back to Sugar. "And what do you mean you're worried about what this place can be?"

As Sugar took the picture from Emery, the door swung open, and in came Sugar's daughter Violet and her new husband, Jackson. Emery's heart about burst when the little girl came barreling toward her, much like her mother did earlier.

Emery was sure it had only been three months since she last saw her in person, but she could swear she'd grown two years' worth in that time. The long, blonde braid going down her back replaced her pigtails. She had on overall shorts with little hiking boots and a tie-dyed T-shirt.

"I missed you, Auntie Em!" she exclaimed as she hugged Emery's neck, her light-blue eyes shining. "Don't go away for so long ever, ever again!" Sugar gave Emery a slight smirk as she shook her head. Kid card wins every time, and Sugar knew it.

"I missed you too, monkey," Emery said as she smiled down at the child. She would do anything for this child . . . anything.

"Welcome back," Jackson said as he hugged her. He was as handsome as ever. Jackson was a big guy standing at six foot five. He had muscles upon muscles from hard work. He neatly trimmed his long, wild beard for the wedding, and he'd kept it that way. It suited him. His long, blond hair was up in a man bun, proving just how much Sugar loved this man. A man bun used to be a deal-breaker for Sugar.

He had dreamy aqua-blue eyes with intense, chiseled features and was just a kind person. If or when the two of them had children, Emery couldn't imagine how beautiful they would be.

"Thanks, it's good to be back," Emery said. She did like Jackson a lot. Sugar was very lucky to find him, and he was lucky as well.

Some might have the opinion that this marriage happened entirely too fast. It only took being around the new little family for a little while to know just how wrong you would be. It was as if they were destined to be together, and it wasn't always perfect, but it was perfect for them.

He noticed Sugar holding the enlarged photograph when he went in for a kiss. "Where'd you find that?

Wow, I haven't seen that picture since Alec sold it to the Farrows."

"Alec took this picture?" Emery asked. Who would have thought? She'd seen some of his pictures here and there, but like everything with Alec, she didn't think he was serious about it. She was almost ashamed of herself for thinking those other shots she saw were probably just luck.

"Oh yeah," Jackson said. "He was really into photography when he was younger. Alec has all kinds of prints like this. In fact, I believe this is the first one he ever sold. Had to be before his junior year, because I left for the service then."

Jackson, Alec, and Madison were all raised together at the grand hotel. Jackson was a later in life child, so as far as generations go, he was on Eric's level. A couple of years older than Madison and Alec he left for the Army before they finished high school.

Emery remembered a picture of Violet, Eric, and Becca that Alec had taken last year while they were ice skating. The photograph was picture perfect, with Eric holding Violet high in the air and Becca looking lovingly at the two from the background.

It's blown up and placed in the family pictures on one of The Lodge's walls. Come to think of it, there are quite a few incredible pictures so amazing people stop to look at them when walking by even though they do not personally know the people in the photos.

She wondered just how many of those were taken by Alec.

Violet interrupted her thoughts. "Auntie Em, you've missed so much! We have a new house, and my kittens are cats, and I went to dance class, and I finished preschool!" she exclaimed without taking a breath.

"I know," Emery said seriously. "I'm here now so you can tell me all about it." Then, taking the little girl's hand, they left the building and headed toward the apartment that would be Emery's home for the foreseeable future.

※

Alec Larsson did not need to deal with this right now. He was behind in his duties for the hotel. So when his sister asked if anyone could pick Emery up, Alec wasn't exactly free but rearranged his schedule. He told himself it wasn't because he wanted to see her as soon as possible after three long months, but because he wanted to help his sister.

Helping his sister by picking Emery up yesterday equaled a very frazzled, running behind Alec.

"Do you hear me, Alec?" Madison, his twin sister and mortal enemy, asked, her probably expensive sky-high heeled shoes tap-tap-tapping at him.

It wasn't always this way—they had been close as children. The divide started in high school. Madison became one of the mean girls, and Alec just didn't have a mean bone in his body. She was still his sister, his twin—he just didn't like her very much during that time.

Her alleged about-face after Alec secretly sent some of her bullying Facebook messages to their parents was short-lived. He wondered if she had found out about him ratting her out. Perhaps that's why she did what she did. For Alec, that was the end of their relationship, and her betrayal was much worse than showing your parents a few Facebook threats.

"Yes, I heard you," Alec said as he separated the last harness for their climbing wall. It had been left a mess and needed to be put back to rights. He knew he needed to talk to some of his employees, but managing people just wasn't a strength of his.

"Grandmother is finally showing up in town, and you want to do a welcome garden party," he said as he threw the harness into the correct pile. "The Snow Valley Hotel will have no part in said garden party."

Madison hated the hotel that Alec and Jackson built. The Lodge property housed many exquisite "cabins," which were more like log mansions. The actual Lodge hosted upwardly mobile people with an eye on being one of the privileged who would one day rent one of those cabins.

The Snow Valley Hotel wasn't anything like the rest of the property. Located on land destroyed by a fire, this property was for people who didn't want to spend time in the actual hotel. They wanted to be climbing the mountain or skiing or fishing or visiting the shops in the square. It was affordable and pleasant and basic.

Jackson had been facing an uphill battle when we first came up with the idea for the deforested property. His father, Paul Anderson, supported him, of course, but Alec's support pushed it through, and Madison would probably hate him until the day he died because of it.

His father could have vetoed it all, being the major shareholder in the business, but he would never do that to Alec. Madison feared it would hurt their brand, but Eric was smart enough to know that diversifying was smart. The cabins had saved the business a time or two when big recessions hit over the years.

A successful businessman rented out one of those luxury cabins from November to January, and he was usually only there three days at most. Alec couldn't imagine having that much money that you could just throw it away like that.

Their small, cost-effective hotel had its place and its own brand. Located a few miles from the main Lodge, no one needed to know they were part of the same company, and who cares if they did? Madison, that's who.

She did have a point, but he would never in a million years admit that to her. The Lodge was a luxury brand. You wouldn't see Tiffany's offering a ten-dollar necklace. Much care was taken to separate the two brands. He couldn't help but smile when he thought his own customers might look down on them being associated with the luxury part of the business.

Still, she didn't need to act like they were trying to always push their way into The Lodge's activities. It was quiet the opposite, actually.

"Great," Madison said, squishing up her pert little nose like she smelled something bad. "You are invited, of course. Not that you have a choice since you're related to her."

"Wouldn't miss it," Alec said with a wide smile. "I am the favorite after all." Few things turned her screws more than the favorite card. The funny thing is that Alec never wanted to be the favorite, and Madison endlessly hated that he was.

"Whatever, just wanted to let you know we didn't need any help from this place," she said as she turned on her heel and started to walk out without saying goodbye.

Jackson entered the rec room just as Madison was leaving. Madison's demeanor changed immediately. "When are you going to give me another niece or nephew?" she teased as she gave his arm a light punch.

"We just got married—give us time," Jackson said. "Are you and Hunter coming next Saturday?"

Alec prayed she would say no. Sugar and Jackson were having a little get-together at their new house next weekend, and he didn't want to spend any of his downtime with his evil twin. Her new boyfriend was a decent dude except for his terrible taste in women.

"We're planning on it," Madison said. They said their goodbyes, and Alec was able to relax.

"A little sibling bonding?" Jackson asked as he helped Alec hang the harnesses up on their hooks.

"Not likely," Alec snorted. "She just wanted to inform me of the garden party for our grandmother and how it would be at The Lodge, and no help would be needed from this dump."

It's not that Alec would want to help plan a garden party. Eric, his father, included the small upstart hotel when there were events at The Lodge, and Madison must have worried he'd want to take part in it.

If he were being honest, he wasn't all that excited to see his grandmother return, and it made him feel terrible. He did love her—she was his grandmother after all—but she had a different way of thinking in which certain people thought they were better than others. It just didn't align with his worldview.

Even this party—Alec knew this party would be like a pristine English garden party thrown for royalty. They hadn't seen their grandmother in over a year. So why couldn't they just have a nice dinner and catch up?

Caitlin Larsson couldn't blame age, or the fact that

that's how things were when she grew up. He knew plenty of grandmothers that didn't look down on anyone. Alec spent a good amount of summers with Jackson at his grandparents' farm in Alabama. His grandmother was warm and funny and didn't think badly of anyone unless they did her wrong.

There was also a reckoning coming. It is no accident that Caitlin is coming back at this time. His father finally told her that Madison, not Alec, was being groomed to take over The Lodge. Naturally, this would not sit well with her, and he'd bet anything that's why she was finally headed home.

It still upset him that she didn't bother coming home when they discovered his sister Sugar. Who doesn't come home to meet their grandchild? Hell, she had a great-grandchild too!

Even though that bothered Alec, nothing upset him more than her not coming when his father married Sugar's mother, Becca. He knew it hurt his father to the quick, even if he wouldn't admit it. Alec's grandmother came home for Christmas every year, except when his father married the love of his life. She was making a statement, and it wasn't a good look for her.

"Oh yes, the return of Caitlin Larsson," Jackson said as he playfully smacked Alec on the back. Jackson lost no love for Alec's grandmother. Caitlin Larsson and her husband, John, always saw the Andersons as a pain in their side rather than business partners. "Good luck with that. What else do you need to do?"

Alec motioned to the general area. "I just need to get everything back in its place." Helmets, gloves, and shoes were haphazardly thrown in their bins.

"We need to talk to Bob about leaving things this way," Jackson said as he began to sort the shoes by size.

Alec grabbed a pair from Jackson. "I'm good here, man. Go be with your family," he said, sidestepping the Bob conversation.

Alec didn't like disciplining people. He just wasn't good at it. The respective families always had their talents, and Alec took after his mother's side. Great with planning activities and events, that part of his family drew people to the property. They were never good at HR-related things.

That would be Madison, all day long.

"Sug, Em, and Violet are knee-deep in a SJL meeting," Jackson said. "I think they are discussing the new building prospects."

When Josh, Sugar's husband, died in a car accident, Emery and Sugar gave his portion of SJL to Violet. They let her participate in meetings from time to time, and sometimes she got a vote. It was essential to Sugar that her daughter witnessed women leading a large company.

"It'll be interesting to see what becomes of it," Alec said. "I'm glad Sugar's putting in an effort and not just renting it out."

Jackson chuckled as he untangled another harness. "Well, I think Sugar wants Emery to open something up there."

"Good luck with that or even getting her to move here," Alec said. "Em is city, not small town."

Jackson looked at Alec and shook his head. "You have met my wife, right? Oh, and your niece? They want her here. Good luck to Emery getting out of that."

Alec laughed. "You've got a point."

After hanging up the last harness and sorting the last set of gloves, Jackson put his arm around Alec's shoulders. "Come on, man, let's go grab lunch," he said. "This is settled good enough."

The pair walked to their home away from home—a large pole barn converted into a man cave of sorts.

"You really do need to talk to Bob," Jackson said. Alec shook his head as he realized his deflection didn't work. "He's taking advantage because he knows you'll put up with it. We can't have that, Alec."

Alec sighed. He hated this part of the business, but he supposed no matter what you do you're never going to like every aspect of your job. "Alright, I'll talk to him."

"Good. You're coming next Saturday too, right?" Jackson asked.

Alec shrugged his shoulders as he opened the door. "We'll see," he said.

Jackson frowned, knowing exactly why Alec might not come. "I was hoping you'd come so Emery would have a partner for some of the games, but it's cool. Matt's coming, so if you can't make it, he'll do. I think they got along well at the wedding too."

They did get along at the wedding, and if Alec remembered right, they danced one and a half times. Thankfully, Eric cut in one of those times, so Alec didn't have to bash in Matt's face. Alec shut the door just a little bit harder than he intended. Oh, he would be at this party, evil twin or not.

Chapter 3

EMERY COLLAPSED ONTO THE COUCH, beat from all the unpacking. Her movers did a fantastic job leaving her to organize the French country-inspired apartment. Emery could not bear disorganization, so she came straight here after leaving Sugar and her little family to put things right.

Most of it was done by the first night she was here, but she still had much to do this morning. Everything was finally in its place just the way Emery liked it. She also spent time at the new office organizing her desk.

Sugar and Violet would be coming over soon to have lunch and talk about the new building. She'd be lying if she said there wasn't a bubble of excitement in her stomach over the idea of what could be done with it. But unfortunately, she never did get an answer from Sugar about why she was worried.

Emery was also expecting more pressure from Sugar to permanently move to Snow Valley. However, Emery had good reasons for holding back. There were friends like Lexis back in her hometown, but she spent most of her time in Vancouver or LA filming holiday movies.

Come to think of it, most of her other friends had started families of their own and were usually tied up.

At times it felt like Emery was fighting a losing battle and fighting it for no good reason. A little part of her felt guilty leaving her parents since her siblings both moved to the other side of the country. Both were more involved with their spouses' families than their own, and Emery wondered how that felt to her parents.

Her phone sprang to life and danced on the table.

Alec's text read: "You, me, bags, S&J's party, kicking butt."

Emery smiled at her phone and texted back: "I have never played bags, so you might want a different partner."

Alec replied: "No way! You have that killer competitive instinct . . . I'll take my chances."

Emery laughed. This was true. Did he know her this well already? She sent a final text before setting her phone back down: "Don't say I didn't warn you."

Even if she considered friendships, of course, her most valuable one was right here. Her circle was just a few tight-knit friends and a bunch of acquaintances. Unfortunately, Sugar grew up being bullied, and Emery hadn't dodged that bullet either. Being mixed race brought out the worst in some people, and she faced a few kids back in the day who seemed offended by her existence.

Quality over quantity was her motto, and it served her well. Sure it might be hard getting Lexis to come out here for a visit, but she could always go there. The new friends she'd made in this small town were so much different than her California acquaintances, and she'd missed them dearly these last three months.

She picked her phone back up and took a quick

picture. Besides working with SJL and mentoring other business, Emery had her own social media presence. Thanks to the exposure from SJL, he personal following was quite large too.

The golden rule for social media is there is no down time. She looked exhausted in the picture, which is just what she wanted. She applied a filter to soften her up just a bit, and posted it to Instagram with the hashtag #movingday.

Hearing a knock at the door that led down to the bakery, Emery called, "Come in." She got up to meet her first guests.

Sugar and Violet came in with something in a glass dish that was undoubtedly delicious if Sugar had any part in making it. Setting it down on the peninsula dividing the kitchen from the great room, Sugar removed the cover to show neat rows of avocado fish tacos.

This woman sure knew the way to Emery's heart. So after gathering some plates and pouring the lemonade, the three partners sat down to business and tacos.

Emery took a bite of her taco and closed her eyes in pure ecstasy. No one cooked like Sugar. Even though baking and sweets were her specialty, she still rocked the savory too. "My god, that's good."

"Thanks," Sugar said. "All right, Violet, so you know we bought two buildings here in the square, right?"

Violet nodded her head yes. "Grandpa says it was a slick move." She giggled.

It wasn't like they bought the properties underneath Eric's nose or anything. The thing is usually owners around the square offer their properties to the Larsson clan before putting it up for sale. They know they'll get a fair price and not have to deal with selling. This time wasn't any different and they went to a Larsson – just a different one from Eric.

"It sure was," Sugar said. Sugar wanted to purchase one, and it was Emery who brought up buying both. "So what I'm proposing to the team is that we open up another business under the SJL umbrella instead of renting it out."

Emery took another bite of her taco and thought about this. Did they need another business?

"And what made you come to this decision?" Emery asked.

Sugar put down her food. "There's been a lot of good things happening around here, in no small part to you, Em," Sugar said. "Once we bought the building, there have been plenty of people coming forward to rent the space, but when I hear about their plans, it just doesn't feel right. More novelty-type shops or T-shirt shops. It doesn't fit with what's been happening around the town."

"I agree," Emery said. The square had leveled up in the last few months. It didn't need to look like a tourist trap. Probably the change in visitors is why the previous owners finally decided to leave. The tourists now wanted more than a poorly put together T-shirt or mug.

Deciding business was better discussed once they were done eating, the trio finished eating their delicious lunch and cleaned up before proceeding.

○≾

Sugar headed to her favorite wingback chair and Emery settled in on the comfortable couch, Violet plopping down next to her.

Emery had to admit that stepping back was a little sad. The company had been their life for so long, and with a tinge in her heart she thought of Josh. Oh, how she loved her friend. If it weren't for him, they wouldn't be in this position in their mid-twenties. Emery knew how fortunate they were to even make these kinds of decisions at such a young age.

Josh was brilliant. His grades won him a scholarship to the private school where he met Emery and Sugar. What they didn't realize was that Josh had always felt inferior because he didn't come from money like most of the kids in the school, and that fact probably drove him as much as it did to make SugarJones.com a success.

Emery witnessed his descent into addiction while Sugar was away in Paris for an internship. After his death, she questioned time and time again if she could have done anything to help him. Josh would drunkenly show up at her dorm room to crash on the floor more times than she could count until she'd finally had enough and put a stop to it.

He turned into someone she did not know but seemed to get better when Sugar returned. Unfortunately, that was short-lived, and once Sugar became pregnant and they married, he dove right back into his old habits. It ended with him driving drunk and crashing after a fight with Sugar. No one knew that fact except the two of them and Jackson. They didn't want Violet to ever find out, so they'd kept it close.

Even after all of that, the two friends still loved Josh, and taking a step back from the company would almost be like finally closing the door on that chapter in their life. It broke her heart just a little, but it was time.

Visiting the office earlier made it all so real. They'd been prepping for this handoff for months, but now they were watching it happen. The part of SJL that involved Josh was now being handed off to others. They needed to process that.

"So what are you proposing?" Emery asked. "We just decided to take a step back, but you want to open another business now?" When the company first bought the building, using it as rental property was the plan. The thought of starting another business was coming from left field.

"I think you need to figure out what kind of business should go there," Sugar said. "With all the work you've put into the town, you know it better than anyone."

"Sug, I don't know about running another business," Emery started to say.

"No, I don't mean we'll be running the day-to-day unless you decide you'd want to with whatever business goes in. It's just that I know you plan on being here for a while since your condo sold, and you're basically homeless. I know how important this town has become to you, so I figured you might want to have a say in what goes in."

It all made perfect sense, and she wasn't wrong. Working with the chamber of commerce and all the small businesses around town was so rewarding. Emery was used to working with them virtually, for the most part, and when she returned and saw the difference she'd made in such a short amount of time, she almost burst with pride. No, she wouldn't want just any old business going in, especially on the corner of the square.

"So basically, figure out what would be a good fit, and then we'd invest and hire people to run it?" Emery asked.

"Pretty much," Sugar said. "I think it's a good move. Businesses support themselves around here. The only time they go up for sale is when someone retires. I think we should go for it."

"I think so too," Emery said, her mind spinning with ideas.

☙

"To our next new adventure," Sugar toasted as they clinked wine glasses, hers filled with sparkling water and Emery's with wine.

"To our next adventure," Emery parroted. Becca and Eric had taken Violet to see the movie in the square that night, so the partners took advantage of the situation to go out. It only seemed fitting to celebrate the next phase of their lives.

There weren't many bars in the small town of Snow Valley, but just a couple blocks away from the square was a comfortable and inviting joint called The Snow Valley Pub & Grub. The structure was a log cabin, and the interior had high beams and a fireplace that stretched to the top of the ceiling. A jukebox stood in the corner, and it had a stage for live bands on the weekends.

A long bar made of dark wood that matched the tables was friendly and inviting, and they had to die for sandwiches and homemade potato chips. Emery and Sugar sat at a table next to one of the large windows that perfectly displayed the far-off mountain peaks.

"Are you sure you just want sparkling water?" Emery asked suspiciously.

"Yeah, I don't feel like drinking," Sugar said.

Emery raised an eyebrow.

"All right, enough with the Spanish Inquisition, I'm knocked up," Sugar said as she blew out an exasperated sigh.

Emery got up and ran around the table to embrace her friend. "Sugar, that's fantastic! I'm so happy for you!"

Sugar hugged her friend back. "Thank you, now sit down before Madison gets here. No one knows but Jackson and yourself. We are going to tell Violet right before we tell everyone at the party next Saturday."

"How are things going for the party?" Emery asked as she returned to her seat. She knew this get-together meant a lot to her friend. It was the first in her new home. Sugar was never a party person, and suddenly Emery realized the main reason for this party.

"Great. Pretty much everything is set. We are going to tell everybody all at once."

"And Madison and Alec are both coming?" Emery asked.

"Yeah," Sugar said. "I don't get those two. I finally told them that if they acted like fools in front of Violet one more time, neither one of them would see her again. At least they are civil while she's around now. She loves them both so much she just didn't understand their constant bickering."

Emery twirled her glass, making a little whirlpool with her wine. "Why do they argue so much? Does anyone know why they hate each other?"

"You got me," Madison said as she sat down, dropping several shopping bags on the ground. She raised her finger and pointed to Emery's glass as the bartender nodded in acknowledgment.

Looking perfectly put together as always, Madison wore her long, dark hair in a high ponytail. Delicate, tasteful diamond earrings studded her ears and a sterling silver Tiffany's Lock necklace adored her neck. An a short-sleeved Argyle sweater with a collar in red, white and blue paired with a white linen pencil skirt and red high heels finished the look.

"Hi, Madison," Emery said as her cheeks blushed. Sugar could have at least let her know she was walking up behind her! "We weren't talking about you—"

"Yes, we were," Sugar interrupted.

Despite Alec's numerous warnings, Sugar and Emery had come to like Madison. Their first experiences with her weren't good, but once they talked it through, they discovered Madison just needed a real friend, something she'd sorely lacked her whole life.

Emery sensed that wasn't the only problem. She didn't take after the Larsson side at all. Her mother was an Olsson, and she was practically her mother's twin. With dark hair and gray eyes, she was beautiful. Her delicate features and petite stature almost gave her an ethereal look, like a magical fairy.

How Emery envied girls like her in high school. Sugar and Emery were both five foot ten by the time they reached high school. Petite, curvy girls like Madison were always the popular ones. Emery felt like an awkward linebacker walking down the glorious halls of high school.

She didn't get the feeling that's how Madison saw things. Emery had heard more than once that her grandfather used to say she was an Olsson, not a Larsson. She can't imagine how hurtful that would be. No wonder she had the reaction she did when she saw Sugar, the dead ringer for John Larsson's mother, show up out of nowhere last fall.

"It's okay. Thank you," she said to the waitress who set down a glass of wine for her. "It's the big mystery of Snow Valley."

Sugar shook her head. "I don't see how it's possible to be a mystery to you when you're involved."

Madison sighed and took a sip of her wine. "Here's what I know. We weren't the best of friends in high school, which was mostly my fault because I was a heinous a-hole."

Sugar and Emery both nodded, knowing this part of the story.

"Alec went to New York for college, and I stayed local," she said. "At Christmas, things were pretty good. We got along, and everything—like the distance gave us a fresh start. It seemed like he was going to give me a second chance, but . . ."

"But," both Emery and Sugar said together when Madison paused.

"But when we both came home for the summer, he had an intense hatred for me. I mean, he didn't like me much during high school, but we could still get along. He hated me suddenly," Madison said, the hurt in her eyes betraying the nonchalant way she spoke those words. "He proved it too. I had a new boyfriend from college, and Alec gave him all my old Facebook posts and told him what a god-awful person I was."

"Wow," Sugar said. "Really?"

This took Emery aback also. She could not imagine Alec being vindictive. She knew there was bad blood between the twins, but Alec was always so laid back and nice. Alec would have had to do that out of pure spite. Never in a millions years would Emery peg Alec for being vengeful.

"Yes, really. He was my first love, and Alec knew it. It turns out he was a bullied kid in high school, so after that, he wanted nothing to do with me," Madison said, her eyes clouding with emotion. "We probably wouldn't have lasted anyway, but for it to end like that? Caused by Alec on purpose? I never asked him why he hated me so much when he returned from college because after he did that to me, I didn't care anymore."

Emery's wheels were turning with this new information. She just couldn't help herself—she'd always been a fixer. When someone she cared for was in pain or had a problem, she was always the first to jump in to help.

Even as disturbing as it was for Alec to act that way, Emery knew him well enough to know something significant would prompt him into such an action. Some misunderstanding was in play because how could Madison not understand what she did to Alec to make him act so out of character?

Sugar gave Emery a knowing look from across the table. She was on board with this too.

"Is this what you were talking about at the wedding?" Sugar asked. Back at Becca and Eric's wedding, Madison commented about Alec not being so sweet and innocent. The two friends wondered about it and couldn't get Madison to spill the beans on what he did to make her say that.

Madison nodded and took a long drink of her wine.

"That's terrible, Mad, really it is. But this all sounds

like it started with a big misunderstanding on Alec's part," Emery said carefully. "Maybe one of your former friends told him something that wasn't true."

How many times did people take a tad bit of truth and run with it, twist it, and turn it into something that creates drama? Emery witnessed it over and over when she was in a sorority. Some people just could not help it. It's like it's in their DNA.

Madison knitted her brows together as she looked at her sister and her new friend. "Don't even think about trying to fix this. There is no fixing it. It's too late."

"Bullshi—," Sugar said, stopping herself nearly too late. She'd been working on her language since she realized her daughter was paying attention. "That's BS. It's never too late—just look at me and my mother."

"Can we just have a nice time today?" Madison pleaded. She was always pretty tough. Tough but fair to her employees, just like her dad, Eric. This subject was getting to her, so Emery decided to help her out.

"So, how's the garden party coming, both of you?" Emery asked as Madison shot her a grateful look.

"Everything is right on point," Madison said. "Thankfully, my mom is helping with most of it. It should meet grandmother's standards."

Sugar made a disgusted face. "I can't believe your mom would help with anything for that woman. Doesn't she ignore her since the divorce?"

Madison sighed. "Yes, she does. She blames my mom for a divorce in the family. 'The first one ever,' as she likes to point out."

Sugar shook her head. "I promised my mom I'd be gracious to the devil's spawn, but it's going to be hard.

If anyone is to blame for years of unhappiness, it's her bastard husband who forced them to marry."

"Sug," Emery said, interrupting her. "I'm sure Madison doesn't need to listen to this all over again."

Their grandfather, John Larson, was a horrible person. Alec and Madison probably knew some of it, but they didn't know the half of it. Eric and Becca suspected he cut the brake lines of a vehicle belonging to a woman threatening the lodge. The man would stop at nothing to put The Lodge under the Larsson's control, so he threatened to hurt Becca and Caitlin if Eric didn't marry Allison Olsson.

Eric was kept in line this way his whole life before his father passed away. Regular beatings were just a part of his childhood, and unfortunately, the man was not above beating his wife or Eric's older sister either.

Eric made it clear that his children did not need to know this side of their family history since it was already painful enough to know their parents had never been in love. Sugar and Emery knew because of Becca, but they both promised never to tell Alec and Madison.

"I'm sorry," Sugar said sincerely. "You were raised with them, so I know you love them."

Emery was very proud of her friend. It was hard keeping secrets with her condition because things seemed to just pop out of her mouth. She hadn't spilled the beans in all this time, and Emery knew this took a lot of work for Sugar.

"It's okay," Madison said. "How's your housewarming party coming, Sugar?" she asked, effectively changing the subject.

"So far, so good," Sugar said. "I've got an incredible

menu planned." Emery smiled. Sugar would think food is the essential part. She did not doubt that the food alone would have people talking for weeks.

"Will Hunter be in town?" Emery asked. Hunter was a judge on the Christmas television show Sugar competed on last year. He came to town asking for Sugar's help last Christmas and instantly connected with Madison.

"He should be," Madison said, looking out the window toward the site where Hunter was renovating a new restaurant. "He's excited about opening a restaurant here. It'll be all his with no partners."

"Now we just need to get someone for Emery," Sugar said slyly, wiggling her eyebrows.

Emery asked for a refill when the server came back to the table. She was going to need it. "Let's not start with that," she said. "Do you know how annoying it is when people so in love think everybody needs to be so in love, and they try and help?"

"Everybody does need to be so in love." Sugar smiled as she took a sip of her drink.

It was laughable. If you picked the romantic out of the two, it always would have been Emery, but things had changed over the years.

"All right, then everyone isn't fortunate enough to find that one person," she said.

"That's BS," Sugar said, catching herself this time. "Screw Quentin."

"Who's Quentin?" Madison asked, confused.

Who is Quentin? Someone Emery wished she'd never met. He was her first everything, really. They met during college orientation and were college sweethearts until her senior year. He came from a very well-to-do family back east, and even though her parents were highly influential and powerful, they were new money.

He was tall with dark, wavy hair and light-green eyes that made her knees weak. His teeth were perfect, except his right eyetooth had just a slight tilt to it instead of being stick straight. Quentin admitted to Emery that this was by design, as people trusted you more if your smile had a minor flaw.

Quentin's whole life was by design. He wanted to be president someday, something his family worked toward for generations. So Emery always saw herself as the first lady, welcoming guests to the white house. She did whatever she could to help him, whether with his studies or encouraging him to do the volunteer activities she knew would help him later.

Then it all fell apart. It still felt like a knife to her chest when she thought about the reason. Emery had been a part of that design until he met her mother.

"He was a jackass that didn't deserve Em," Sugar said, breaking Emery from her thoughts. "Since then, she only dates boring idiots she knows she won't get attached to."

"Sugar!" Emery exclaimed. "That is not true." Sugar claimed this time and time again, but Emery refused to believe it. She just looked for someone with the right fit, which sometimes didn't include chemistry and romance.

"What. Ever. One word: Todd. Enough said." Sugar was referencing Emery's last boyfriend. He was about as interesting as watching paint dry. "I just want to see you happy. Matt's going to be at the party, you know."

Emery laughed. Knowing Sugar, this was all part of her elaborate let's-get-Emery-to-move-to-Snow Valley plan.

"What?" Sugar asked. "He's a great dude."

"Are you forgetting about Gina?" Madison asked. "No man is worth dealing with her."

Emery met both Matt and Gina at Sugar's wedding. Matt was a handsome police officer in town and had been in the military with Jackson when they were younger. He reached about six feet two in height, and with hazel-green eyes and jet-black hair, Matt turned a few heads in his day.

Gina Romano just grabbed Emery's heart. Matt's best friend since childhood, the poor girl had it bad for him. Everyone seemed to know this except for Matt. Emery doubted this would be a case where Matt realized Gina was his one true love, so eventually, Gina was going to get her heart ripped out, and Emery wanted no part of it.

"Well, I would mention the obvious—Alec —but I don't want to trigger you," Sugar said to her sister.

"Much appreciated," Madison said while toasting Sugar.

Emery sighed and took another sip of her wine. She wished they would all just let it be.

Chapter 4

THE FOLLOWING DAY, EMERY AWOKE EARLY, so she threw on her workout clothes and set out for a run after making a quick smoothie. She wasn't ecstatic about exercise like Sugar could be, but she knew it was a necessary evil. Bounding down the back stairs, she ran to the end of the buildings, then headed back to the inner square.

It was a great place to run if you woke early before all the shoppers were out. As she jogged past all the shops, she mentally cataloged them in her mind. The air smelled of fresh flowers, and just a bit of a chill was in the air, which would be chased away by the rising sun.

The square housed several restaurants. Romano's Pizza was a popular destination for locals and tourists alike. Gina's family owned the thriving restaurant, which like The Lodge, had been around for a couple of generations.

A small sandwich shop and an ice cream parlor were other businesses that counted the square as their home. The town hall was in one of the more significant corner buildings like Emery and Sugar owned. It was directly across from theirs, actually, and the police department shared the space.

Emery ran past the law office of Calvin, Lewis, and Smith, a small convenience store, the local pharmacy, and a local tour company that took people out on hikes or drives through the mountains. Having a town utterly devoid of a Starbucks or a Walmart was strange, but in a good way.

Her talented friend Holly owned Mountain Top Flowers, another shop on the square. She saw movement inside the store on her second pass, so she decided to stop by after her workout was complete.

Emery's feet rhythmically pounded the sidewalk to the beat of the song playing in her air pods. The square had a good mix of stores already—the corner building needed to bring something new to the table. But what was missing?

She jogged past the nail salon, a jewelry shop, and a dress shop . . . the square had great diversity.

She slowed to a walk, took her water bottle out of her small backpack, and took a long drink. Then, wiping the sweat off her forehead, she took a good look around. There were many family activities in the square, from the movie nights to the newly installed splash pad, which was an immediate hit. Maybe the new space could be something family friendly.

Maybe they could turn the building into an escape room? Too gimmicky. The charm of this town came from the fact that generations of families put love into their businesses like Sugar's bakery and Gina's pizza place. An escape room would do great right now, but Emery couldn't see it as a business for the long haul.

The only reason Sugar and Emery were able to purchase the two buildings was because their children and grandchildren didn't want to run the businesses. Most had a long history, and a good portion of them were owned by one family since the 1940's, when it all was built.

She needed to respect that legacy, while making it her own. Emery cared deeply for these people and it was important she get this right.

Slowing down as she came to the flower shop again, Emery peered into the window. A little boy about Violet's age with bright-red hair popped up and gave Emery an enthusiastic wave. She watched as he yelled something inaudible, and his mother, Holly, with the same bright-red hair, appeared.

Opening the door, she immediately gave Emery a big hug.

"Oh, I'm all gross from running," Emery warned, but Holly hugged her anyway.

"I heard you were back in town," Holly said as she led the way into her store.

Another family legacy, Mountain Top Flowers, was handed down to Holly from her great-aunt. It was a godsend as her husband had just walked out on her and her son, Sam.

If Emery ever needed somewhere to go to cheer herself up, this was the place. Of course, there were flowers everywhere, and Holly was incredibly talented with her arrangements. She was an artist. Some might think the shop was a bit busy with every square inch covered in flowers, but Emery loved it.

"Hi, Sam," Emery said and smiled at the shy little boy hiding behind his mom's legs.

"What do you say to Emery, Sam?" Holly prompted.

"Hi, Miss Emery," Sam said and then quickly hid his face again.

"Come on back," Holly said as she led Emery to her workshop behind the front counter. "I just made some coffee. Would you like some?"

Nodding in the affirmative, Emery followed Holly back and took a seat at a big butcher block covered with yellow roses, baby's breath, blue hydrangea, and white lilies. Paired with green foliage, there were a few bouquet arrangement among the pile of happy flowers.

"It's missing something," Holly called out as she poured them each a cup of coffee.

"Thank you," Emery said as Holly sat a cup of coffee in front of her. "Hold on a second."

Emery got up and went back into the main part of the flower shop. A particular flower caught her eye when she walked in, and it would look great in the arrangement. With spikes of a beautiful, vibrant blue bell-shaped flowers, it would blend harmoniously with the rest of the flowers.

"What about these?" Emery asked.

"Belladonna delphinium," Holly answered, holding one by its delicate stem. "This is going to be the flower arrangement for the garden party next weekend, and these are just what I needed. Thank you."

Emery watched as Holly hand expertly placed a belladonna stems here and there, bringing the bouquet to life.

"These will be perfect," Emery said, taking a sip of her coffee. "The arrangement reminds me of a beautiful, blue summer sky."

A monstrous smile broke out on Holly's face. "That's

the exact look I was trying to achieve! You have a great eye, Emery."

That wasn't the first time Emery had heard something like that. Her art professor always told her that her penchant for picking out artwork was second to none, and she interned at an art gallery on his insistence.

"Thank you," Emery said. "These are going to look beautiful. Has there been any change in the Madison/Holly deep freeze?"

Holly was one of the girls Madison bullied in high school, and Holly had bullied Madison in grade school. Emery thought it would be nice if her friends could all get along, but that didn't seem to be the case here. Madison had been brutal to Holly and never really apologized.

Madison did throw all The Lodge's floral needs to Holly's shop, which made it instantly successful. It was struggling when she first inherited the business and was now thriving with Madison's intervention. It may not be an apology, but it put food in Sam's mouth. That had to count for something.

"Don't start, Em," Holly said as she scooped up the flowers on the table and moved them to the side. "So, any news on what's going in the corner building?"

The people who owned businesses in the square and the surrounding areas were very aware of the empty building. Even though the town would never approve of a large corporate entity inhabiting the space, people still worried.

"Not yet," Emery said. "We are thinking of opening something ourselves. Sugar wasn't happy with the people who've tried to rent it so far."

Holly let out a massive sigh. "Oh, thank you. Most

peeps around here will be relieved to hear that. I still remember the controversy when the Farrows changed over to the novelty store. My Aunt was enraged."

"What was it before that?" Emery asked. As far as she knew, it was always a big novelty shop filled with souvenirs.

"It was a craft store," Holly said as she began placing flowers in a vase, a riot of blue exploding in front of Emery's eyes. "They also took people's crafts on consignment and sold them. That quilt came from there, I believe."

The quilt hung on the wall opposite Emery, and she got up to take a closer look. Hand-stitched, each square had a different flower in shades of purple. In addition, hand-embroidered flowers were in each of the four corners in a lovely shade of peach. It was beautiful.

"Why the change, I wonder?" Emery said more to herself than to Holly.

"Things just changed," Holly said, shrugging her shoulders. "People weren't as crazy about handcrafted items as they are now. You have no idea how you've helped this town, do you?"

Emery blushed at the compliment. "Of course I realize people weren't the most current with social media . . ." she started to say.

"It's not just that," Holly said. "Listen, I know I've had my share of problems with the Larsson's in my day, but that was nothing compared to what the people in this town faced with John Larsson. A big part of the reason why the next generation didn't take over was because they didn't want to be under John's thumb."

"Yes, but he passed over ten years ago," Emery said.

"Yes, he did, and no one knew if they wouldn't get more of the same from Eric. I tell you what, I wouldn't have come back here if I wasn't desperate. I would have put this place up for sale and stayed in Arizona."

"People have to realize that Eric is way different than his father, right?" Emery questioned.

Holly's fingers worked fast placing the Belladonna here and there, bringing the arrangements to life. "Memories are long, Emery. I thought all these buildings would end up being bought out by the Larssons, but you've stopped that. People have faith they can have a future here and have it without walking on eggshells for the Larssons. You did that."

"Well I'm glad I could help," Emery said. She desperately wanted to change the subject. Emery wasn't naïve and knew the town had history with Sugar's family. There was no changing it, but they could all move forward.

"So, are you going to Sugar's party Saturday?" she asked.

Holly laughed. "I will if Sugar hasn't picked out some guy for me. I swear she's been on a cupid tear ever since she got married."

"Preaching to the choir," Emery said. "Now that I'm back in town, maybe you'll be off the hook for a little bit."

Holly bent forward over the table, leaning toward Emery. "Sugar's even said maybe you and Alec could get together." Holly let out a laugh. "I told her you are not that stupid."

"No, I would never risk our friendship for a man," Emery responded. "Did you ever date him back in the day?"

"No way," Holly said. "I know plenty that did, though. No good can come from dating Alec. He couldn't get serious with a woman to save his life."

"Alec is a good friend, but—"

"Oh no, I didn't mean he wasn't a good person," Holly interrupted. "He's never led people on or acted like he wanted more just to get in someone's pants, but he doesn't get serious, and you don't seem like a hookup kind of girl."

"No, I'm not," Emery said. "At this point, I'm not any kind of girl. I need to get my life in order before I even think about a relationship."

"Amen," said Holly. "Good luck convincing Sugar of that."

Good luck, Emery thought. She'd need it.

○₹

Emery took a seat next to Becca across from the large splash pad. It was the perfect replacement for the ice-skating rink during the warmer months. Children laughed, ran, and played as the water randomly shot out from the ground.

She was so happy when Becca called and said she was taking Violet to the splash pad. Truth be told, Emery didn't know what to do with herself. She'd always been so busy. This morning when she woke up she immediately grabbed her laptop to log in and handle SJL business, forgetting it wasn't her job anymore.

For so much of her life, work was the first thing she did when she woke up. But, unfortunately, a lot of days, it was the last thing she did too. She squeezed in some life here and there, but her work/life balance was heavily tilted to work.

She waved at Violet, who was currently screeching with the other children, stopping for only a second to wave back. She noticed Sam's babysitter across the pad, and Sam was running right along with Violet, having a great time.

Maybe her current idea could bring as much joy to the town as this splash pad did. Emery was grateful to bounce it off Becca before talking to Sugar. This was more in Becca's realm of expertise, and Emery knew for certain Becca would tell her the truth.

Becca looked lovely with her long, blonde hair in its signature messy bun, oversized white Jackie O sunglasses, and a cool sundress filled with yellow flowers. She simply glowed with happiness; marriage suited her well.

"It's so good to have you in town." Becca smiled. "Do you have everything you need?"

Emery smiled at Becca. She was always the mother hen. "Yes, everything is wonderful. The movers did a great job, and my car was delivered yesterday."

"Perfect," she said. "How are you doing with all the business changes? Sugar has the bakery to keep her hopping, but you are used to running full speed. Are you dealing with everything okay?"

Becca always knew the right thing to say. "I'm okay for the most part," Emery said. "I didn't realize just how big of a change it would be. My clients here are almost self-sufficient, so I'm wrapping all that up now. I guess I need another project until I figure out what I want to do long-term."

"Sugar said you all are going to start some kind of

business in the new building," Becca said. "Any ideas for that yet?"

Emery looked out at the square. From their vantage point, they were right in the middle. There were obviously tourists, but so many more people from the community. She loved this feeling of belonging.

"I'm glad you asked that," she said. "I really wanted to run this by you and get your opinion. I haven't even told Sugar yet."

Becca smiled at Emery, revealing a little dimple above her lip, just like Sugar. "I'm honored. What's your idea?"

Emery took a deep breath. "An art gallery. A mix of local talent, and once I get going, maybe more nationally known artists. And I want all kinds of art. Painting, glass, sculpting, pottery, photography. I even want handmade items like quilts and embroidery. I think that's art too."

Becca took Emery's hand and gave it a squeeze. "Emery, that's a fantastic idea! An art gallery is just what the square needs!"

Her blood was pumping now, and she was so excited the words just came tumbling out. "I also want to have an artist residency. Maybe offer them six months at the gallery. You should see the back area, Becca! It's so large that it could easily house a studio for all kinds of mixed media. The corner has amazing light with windows on both sides. It would be easy to make a studio apartment on one side and a studio on the other."

Becca put her arms around Emery's shoulders and gave her a squeeze. "That's my Em, always wanting to help others," she said. "I think you have outdone yourself with this idea, Miss Copper."

Emery's smile faltered a bit. "I don't know how

fruitful it'll be money-wise," she said. "I worked in galleries during college, and without a big name, turning a profit is tough."

"Ah yes, but it seems you will also be selling more affordable pieces of art. A lot of the big galleries look down their noses at crafts," Becca said. "I think you need not worry about a profit just yet and go with your heart."

"I'll try," Emery said. "I am Laura and Avery Cooper's daughter, you know."

Becca threw her head back and laughed. "Yes, I know, which is why I know there's no way this place isn't going to turn a profit."

Emery smiled. Becca was right. She was a Cooper, and this would be successful.

"Besides, it's lovely when a childhood dream comes true," Becca said.

Emery tilted her head. "What do you mean?"

"Don't you remember? Sugar used to draw those crazy pictures and you would tape them to the wall of your art gallery."

"Oh my goodness, I totally forgot about that," Emery said.

The two of them played all kinds of pretend games, and she loved when they played art gallery. She would give Becca tours explaining the artwork on the wall. Perhaps this was all meant to be.

CR

Emery smiled as she watched the swirling red, white, and blue flowers dancing in the Snow Globe Café window. Out of all the businesses in the square this was the most recognizable. Made of the same smooth grey stone as the rest of the buildings it stood out because of the large snow globe window, which was always decorated to the appropriate upcoming holiday.

Holly made flower arrangements sometimes for the window, and the fourth of July explosion seemed to be her handywork.

"Hey Em," Alec lazily drawled. She hadn't even noticed him approaching and looking at him she wondered how that was even possible. His blonde locks were longer than she remembered, and those curls just above the collar of his preppy blue polo was begging to be touched.

"Hi Alec," she answered, turning her attention back to the window. She could feel heat coming to her cheeks as she wondered what the hell was wrong with her. This was Alec for goodness sake.

"I have to run but I wanted to tell you that you look lovely today, Miss Cooper," he said as he did a deep bow.

If her cheeks weren't red before they certainly were now. "Thank you," she said but his form was already retreating.

No wonder the women of this town didn't stand a chance with him.

She heard the bells on the front door jingle as Sugar poked her head out. "It's nice, isn't it?" she asked.

Sugar held open the door and Emery walked in. "I love it."

She loved this whole café. The first thing you viewed when you walked in was a large picture of Sugar's grandfather and his first wife. Three smaller pictures butted up against the large photo – one with Sugar's grandfather and her mother Becca, one with Becca and Sugar as a toddler, and one with Sugar and Violet. It perfectly set the stage for a warm and inviting experience.

A long bakery case ran the length of the wall, and Emery was disappointed to see it was empty. Noticing her friend's disappointment, Sugar gestured for her to follow her around back to the kitchen.

It was eerie seeing the bakery this quiet, but it was closed on Sunday and Sugar normally used this time to develop recipes if Jackson was busy at work. With Violet busy with Becca in the square, Sugar had the time to get her creative on.

Emery sat down at the large butcher block in the center of the room, and Sugar produced one of the most mouth-watering brownies Emery ever witnessed.

"Is this a S'mores brownie?" Emery asked. There was a delicate graham cracker crust, then gooey brownie, then torched marshmallow, which if Emery knew anything, she knew it was homemade. Sugar didn't use pre-packaged ingredients ever.

"Yup," Sugar said. "Fall is coming and that's all anyone wants. S'mores this, S'mores that. Usually, I can't stand freakin' S'mores but this time S'mores seem to be my big craving."

Emery smiled as she watched her friend lay a protective hand on her belly. When she was pregnant with Violet, she couldn't get enough cherry pie, any kind of cherry pie, whether homemade or fast food. She lived on it the first few months.

As she bit into what could only be described as pure heaven, she silently thanked Sugar's small fetus. "OMG," Emery said as soon as her mouth wasn't glued together with chocolate marshmallow goodness. "No matter what

I do or how much I beg do not give me another ones of these!"

Sugar laughed as she poured her friend a glass of milk. "I'll take that as a compliment," she said as she sat the milk down in front of Emery. "Have you thought anymore about the new building?"

"Yes actually," Emery said after taking a refreshing drink of the ice-cold milk. "It's funny you should ask because I was just speaking with your mom about it."

"Hold on one second," Sugar said as she reached into the pocket of her apron and handed Emery an envelope. "Note that it's completely sealed and then open it."

Curiosity ran through Emery's features as she turned the white envelope over and opened it. Reaching inside she pulled out what looked to be a recipe card. Written on it were two words: art gallery.

Emery's brows knitted together to form a little V between her eyebrows. "How did you know?"

"Ha!" Sugar said with a brilliant smile. "You are not the only one who pays attention you know. I know you just as well as you know me."

Emery shook her head with her own brilliant smile on her face. Back when they first came to this little town, Emery knew Sugar would move here and had everything planned out for her before she realized it.

"I never had a doubt that you didn't know me," Emery said. "Your mother just reminded me how we used to play art gallery. Is that why you guessed that?"

"I guess partially," Sugar said as she took a bite of her own S'mores brownie. "Em, you always say that you're not an artist but you are. SJL? You always knew the perfect picture, the perfect video to post. Without that we could have been one hit wonders. One viral video and that's it. You just have that knack for knowing what looks good. It'll suit the new art gallery well."

"This doesn't mean I'm moving here," Emery said.

"Sure, Em" Sugar said as she winked at Emery. "Keep telling yourself that."

ॐ

Emery checked herself in the mirror one last time before heading out to Sugar's party. Wearing a peach sundress, Emery felt fresh and summery. It was a pale shade of peach with mint green accents, her favorite color combination. Yellow flowers also dotted the dress, and it was close-fitting from the bodice to the waist and then flared out, hitting just above the knee.

Despite the warning to the contrary, the weather had stayed beautiful all week, and the sun shone brightly every day. Finally, they were far enough into the summer that they didn't need to worry about winter rearing its ugly head for one last hurrah.

For comfort's sake, she chose flat, yellow strappy sandals and a yellow bag. She blew out the curl in her hair until it cascaded in dark, sexy waves down her back, with a mint green headband pulling it away from her face. The headband complimented her eyes, and the peach dress complimented her mocha skin tone perfectly. The necklace she wore—a heart locket given to her by Violet, containing a picture of the two of them—was one of her favorite possessions.

A little bit of mascara and lip gloss finished off the look. Emery grabbed her keys, and threw them and her purse into her large Coach bag. Sugar insisted she stay the night just in case she had a couple of drinks. Emery couldn't argue with her there. After Josh, they both made a solemn vow to each other that they would never ever drink and drive, even if it was just a couple of drinks.

She took the back stairs down from her apartment two at a time, happily humming to herself. Unlike Sugar, Emery was a social animal. She loved parties and get-togethers. After the week she'd had, a nice fun party was just the ticket. Her sleek convertible roared to life, and she pulled out, heading toward The Lodge's property.

Back in her element, she was going full speed ahead with this art gallery plan and meticulously researched and planned all week long. With Sugar's approval, Emery took the idea and ran with it. This was all so unlike her. Sugar was the one who always leaped before she looked. This was foreign to Emery, and she had to admit—it was exhilarating.

In the meantime, she'd set up shop in her new office at SJL. She had to admit it was nice going to a place every day to work. It would sound funny to most people, but she'd never had that. Most were blown away that they'd built this massively successful company all from home, but they had.

Emery was a structured, disciplined person, so working from home didn't present any problems. Her main concern was *not* working while at home. When your job is only a mouse click away, it becomes hard to separate work from life. Emery needed to work on that whole work/life balance thing big time.

She tried her hardest to just work office hours, but the new gallery needed a lot of work. She needed to make the cosmetic improvements, find artists to fill the gallery, and find a way to get people excited about a gallery in a very tiny town in Colorado that wasn't near all the major cities.

Pulling down the road leading to The Lodge always took Emery's breath away. It was so gorgeous, this majestic log structure peering out of the woods. Three families had come together to build this, and the originals sure knew what they were doing.

It easily could have looked like a monstrosity and stuck out like a sore thumb, but from the gentle peaks of the roof to the large glass windows, it looked like mother nature herself built this lodge and placed it right here. It was even grander at night when it was all lit up. The sky was always full of stars with no city lights around, and The Lodge looked like a star shining right here on Earth.

She turned down The Lodge's service road, knowing that led to all the family homes. She drove past the massive house where Alec and Madison were raised. Their mom and her wife lived there now. After a minute or so, she drove past Becca and Eric's place. It was much smaller than the grand family home, and she knew that's how they liked it.

Driving a little farther, she reached Sugar and Jackson's home. Another log cabin, she knew Jackson and his father gutted it and started over. The little three-bedroom ranch in the woods was adorable, its slanting roof and rounded door making it look straight out of a fairy tale.

Parking her car, she noticed Becca and Eric leaving the house.

"Emery!" Becca said as she pulled her into a hug. "It's so good to see you!"

Emery hugged her right back. "It's good to see you too," she said with a big smile.

Once Becca released her, Eric stepped in to give her a big bear hug. "Good to have you back home," Eric said with a wink.

"Ahh, not you too!" Emery laughed. She popped the trunk to her car, revealing the boxes of desserts she'd picked up for Sugar from the café.

"I got this," Eric said as he started scooping up boxes.

"Let's go for a walk," Becca said, looping her arm with Emery's.

Emery gave Becca a confused look but walked on with her, curious as to what this was about.

"I've been thinking about the new gallery," Becca said as they walked a small trail leading away from the house. "You are going to do such a fantastic job! What plans do you have so far?"

Becca was also a talented artist who had illustrated all her children's novels. Their mutual love of art was one of the things that tied the two of them together.

"I'm fortunate that the interior is already a big blank canvas," Emery said. "I have a few artists in mind to feature from back home, and I've put the word out around town for any local artists. What I really need is to hook a big name to put the gallery on the map, especially since this town is just a little pin prick on the map compared to big cities."

Becca listened intently and Emery secretly wished her mom were more interested. Her parents called her on her weekly call, Wednesday at 8:00 p.m. California time and she told them her news. She knew she was a running appointment in her parents' calendar, just as her sister was on Tuesday and her brother on Thursday.

Oh, her mom listened when Emery called to tell her the news. She did not ask questions or offer suggestions, just congratulated her and told her to be sure to tell her assistant when she knew the day of the opening and they'd try their best to make it.

"So what's the plan?" Becca asked as they sat on a fallen tree that was carved into a bench. "One big opening with a big artist and then cater to smaller artists?"

Emery spent much of this week thinking about this very topic. "I want a hybrid opening," she said. "I'd love to have a few items to display that will make people want to come, but then have small displays of up-and-coming artists to give them exposure to high-end clients."

She sighed. "Now I just have to figure out how to do that." She could see the logistics in her head, but it was hard to pick artists until she snagged someone big. The associated smaller artists needed to be in the same vein of work or theme as the prominent artist.

There were also the logistics of when the building would be ready. She still didn't have a name for the gallery, and it would be at least a couple of months to get the moveable half walls she wanted. With those she would be able to configure the gallery to suit each artist.

"Well, I know I'm not a famous artist or anything but I do have some of the original illustrations I made for *Beatrice the Butterfly*," Becca said. "I'd be happy to showcase them in your new gallery."

Emery sat there on that log in the woods surrounded by nature's beauty utterly speechless.

"You don't have to, it was just a thought," Becca said when Emery still hadn't responded.

"No no, I'm just completely and totally at a loss for words," Emery said. "That is such a generous offer. I just . . . can't believe it."

Becca patted Emery's knee and laughed. "It's not that big of a deal. I've been wanting to auction some of them off for my charity and thought perhaps part of it could go into your fund for the resident artists you plan to bring on."

Emery knew this was a huge deal. Beatrice was a cultural phenomenon on par with all the big children's characters. Not only were there Becca's books, but there were also cartoons and movies and merchandise. Having her original illustrations at her opening? It would make her gallery in one night.

"Yes, it is," Emery said. "Of course I would love to have your illustrations at my gallery opening! My mom may kill me for being the one to get you to put them out there."

Laura Cooper, Emery's mom and Becca's agent, tried unsuccessfully over the years to get Becca to show and sell her original illustrations.

Becca laughed. "Are you kidding? She's the one who suggested it."

Emery felt a lump form in her throat as she tried her darndest to swallow it down. "Really?" she managed to say.

"Oh, Em," Becca said as she put her arm around her adopted daughter. "Your mom is your biggest cheerleader."

Becca nodded. "I know." Over the years random

LEAVING HOME

people would gush about how proud Laura Cooper was of Emery. She just never really heard it straight from her mom and it always got to her when other people said these things.

"Some people have a harder time showing emotions, yes?" Becca asked her, giving her shoulder a squeeze.

"Yes, they do," Emery said. "Becca, I can't thank you enough for this opportunity."

"Oh, sweetheart you thank me every day that you are part of my family," she said as she stood up. "Come on now, we better get back before that daughter of mine sends out a search party."

Taking Becca's outstretched hand, she stood up too. A million ideas were now swirling in her head about the accompanying artists for the grand opening that would mesh well with Becca's illustrations. Emery's childhood dream was becoming a reality and she never imagined it would be this exciting.

☙

Alec pulled up to Sugar and Jackson's house and the party was in full swing. His last group's nature walk went way over time, but he didn't mind. He loved showing this land that he loved so dearly to others. Children and adults alike were usually left awestruck after one of the hikes—astonished by these mountains' beauty and majestic wonder. Alec loved every minute of it.

Planning and executing events was his specialty. He inherited this from his mother's side of the family. When the three families came together to build this business all those years ago, the Olsson side was social. They had the significant money contacts and they knew how to throw an event. An Olsson never met a stranger.

When Jackson wanted to build the new hotel, it was an out for Alec. It was always expected that he would take over The Lodge and the luxury cabins, especially when he didn't end up majoring in photography when he went to college.

He was well aware that he could walk away from it all, and his father would not mind one bit. Eric never pressured him about the business, unlike his grandfather John. That man seemed to press upon Alec the legacy that was his and how it was his responsibility to fulfill it.

This probably wasn't how John figured he'd fulfill his legacy, but it fit Alec like a glove. If he wasn't going to live one dream, this was a pretty good second best. At the Snow Valley Hotel, Alec was free to take over all the events and activities, and he led many of them.

Madison would be free to run The Lodge and the cabins, and that's really how it should have always been. He may not get along with his sister, but she was born to do that job. Growing up he used to feel so bad because she tried so hard to be seen by their grandfather.

People were where they needed to be no matter what the previous generations thought. Times have changed and women are more than capable of running something this big. Grandmother Caitlin would probably have much to say on this when she came into town, but he'd deal with that as it came. Thankfully he knew his parents, along with his stepparents, would always have both his and Madison's back.

He walked around back as most of the action seemed to be outside. The large brick patio ran the length of the ranch-style log cabin, and it took Jackson and Alec almost two whole weekends to install what was now lit up with what seemed to be a million fairy lights. The ornate wood table and chairs were joined by two long temporary tables covered with flowery tablecloths. One was set up with chairs, and the other set up with all his sister's goodies.

Alec and his sweet tooth were heading on over to crush those mini pies, cakes, and cookies when he was stopped by his own heart.

"Uncle Alec!" Violet shouted as she ran to him. "I've been waiting forever for you to get here!"

Alec laughed and picked up his little niece. "I am so sorry to keep you waiting! I had work to do but I'm here now," he said as he blew a raspberry on her cheek.

He didn't know you could love another human this much before Sugar and Violet came into his life. Alec had never been around children except for when he was a child himself. Violet had straight-up stolen his heart and wrapped him around her little finger in one fell swoop.

"I'm going home with Grams and Grandpa soon," she said, sounding a little disappointed.

Alec set her back on her feet. "Well, we'll just have to make the most of it now. How about we smash the dessert table?"

He looked around the party and waved to several friends as he downed a mini key lime pie. Bored with eating, Violet abandoned him quickly. He finally laid eyes on Emery, standing on the edge of the patio sipping a drink.

Of course she looked gorgeous, and of course that jerk Matt was standing right next to her and she was smiling at him. She had on a sundress with little strappy shoulder things that drove Alec insane, and they looked deep in conversation.

I mean, what did Matt have going for him? Yes, he was a decorated war hero and a police officer. Alec supposed if you were a female, you might be into that tall, dark, and handsome look. But he was too serious for Emery. She needed someone who would make her take chances and experience new things.

She needed someone like him. Well, not him—that was impossible. Relationships were not Alec's forte. Still, he was in a slump, but he chalked that up to his sister stealing his wingman. It was not even remotely possible Alec's sex life had stalled because he met a certain lady with hazel eyes and the most beautiful mouth he had ever seen.

Nope. It had nothing to do with that. It also did not mean he couldn't care for her and worry about her well-being, and Matt would end up boring her to death.

Like an angel from the heavens, Gina appeared just in time, inserting herself between Emery and Matt. Alec would have to tip her double the next time he got a pie from her family's pizza place. He wasn't grateful for his own nefarious reasons, mind you. He would just hate to see Emery die of boredom.

CR

"I'm so glad it's working out well for the station," Emery said as she smiled at the handsome police officer. She met Matt Morelli at the wedding, and he questioned how social media could help the Snow Valley PD.

LEAVING HOME

Together they worked up a plan to show the humorous side of police work and the community responded enthusiastically. It was a hit, and the police department was lucky to find that one of their dispatchers could have a side gig as a comedy writer.

"There you are," Gina said as she came between the two, linking arms with Matt. "I've been looking for you everywhere."

Matt, oblivious as ever, smiled at Gina. "Emery and I were just talking about the social media project for the office. Emery, have you met Gina?"

How could she not have met Gina? Every time Matt tried to talk to her she popped up. "Yes I have. I think I missed your pizza almost as much as my friends when I was back in California," Emery said kindly.

"Thank you," Gina said with a tight smile. "I think you've even made a believer out of my stepfather with the social media work."

"Hey, Em," Alec interrupted as he put his arm around her shoulders and gave her his slow, sexy grin. "I'm here—no need for you to be sad anymore."

Emery rolled her eyes. "Oh, I've been waiting with bated breath," she said as she slipped her arms around his waist and exaggeratedly batted her eyelashes at him.

Alec looked fantastic with a fitted light-blue shirt that made his eyes even more piercing and white, knee-length shorts.

"Hi, Matt. Gina. Are you having fun?" Alec asked.

Gina visibly relaxed when Alec walked up and put his arm around Emery. She couldn't help but have compassion for the woman. It was all so obvious. Emery wondered if Gina had friends to gently lay it all out for her.

"We're having a great time." Gina beamed.

Alec pointed at the bag game set up in the yard. It was nearing dusk now, but they'd lit up the entire backyard. "What do you say to a friendly game of bags?" he asked. "Em and I versus you two?"

Matt smiled at Gina. "They don't know who they're challenging, do they?"

The foursome headed toward the bag game when the music stopped and Sugar, Jackson, and Violet appeared in the middle of the patio. "Can we have your attention?" Jackson asked.

Little Violet looked like she was about to jump out of her skin. "We'll be right back," Emery said to Matt and Gina as she grabbed Alec's hand. "You don't want to miss this!"

Alec gave her a quizzical look and followed her to the inner circle surrounding the couple and their daughter.

Emery knew this was coming, long before Sugar told her she was pregnant. Violet being an only child was something Sugar hated, so the minute she married Jackson, Emery knew they would be trying for another child. Jackson had the perfect disposition for a father. He was patient and kind, and even though he could be a disciplinarian when he needed to, it about killed him when he did.

"First we'd like to thank everyone for coming," Sugar said.

"While this is a housewarming, that's not all it is," Jackson said.

Emery's eyes went to Becca and Eric, and Paul and Yvonne, Jackson's parents.

"We're having a baby!" Violet shouted with her tiny

hands clenched in fists, unable to contain her excitement anymore.

Becca's hand flew to her mouth as Eric embraced her. Yvonne had tears in her eyes as she went to embrace first Sugar, and then Jackson. Jackson was born late in life so this was incredibly heartwarming for them. Paul picked up Violet and danced around merrily.

Alec took Emery by the shoulders. "Em, we're pregnant!" Alec said excitedly as he scooped her up in a big hug and swung her around in circles. "It's an exclamation point day!"

Emery's head tilted back as she laughed. Things were just perfect.

"What on earth is an exclamation point day?" she asked as he twirled her around.

"When every sentence you say should end in an exclamation point because it's so damn wonderful," he said, his blue eyes shining with happiness.

Emery's hazel eyes mirrored his happiness. She could get used to exclamation point days.

ஓ

"I told you I never played the game before," Emery said. Matt and Gina had wiped the floor with them.

It surprised her how much she enjoyed Gina's company once she thought Emery was with Alec. Gina was fun and smart as a whip. Emery felt compassion for the girl and decided then and there she would try and befriend her. She got the feeling that Gina didn't have many friends and could use one.

Emery and Alec had wandered away a bit from the

party and found themselves on a couple of swings Jackson installed for Violet. They could still see the party in full motion, but it was just far enough away that things were a little more peaceful and not so loud.

"Yeah, but I didn't realize you'd be so epically bad," Alec teased as Emery swung over and bumped him sideways. "I'm also really proud of you tonight."

Emery gave him a questioning look as they both pumped their legs, swinging higher.

"Not once have you asked why I haven't uploaded the climbing schedule for next month."

"Ha! That's not my problem anymore, Mister," she said as the wind blew her hair back, making her feel like she was a little kid again. "You know they hired a full-time social media person. My work with The Lodge and Snow Valley Hotel is complete."

Eric had been a tough sell in the beginning, but he eventually took on Emery as a consultant. The numbers spoke for themselves. Ever since building up their social media presence, they were booked solid during the holidays and almost wholly booked all summer, which was unheard of.

Her work with the town was almost coming to an end too. Her side business for social media marketing was more about getting people started and then letting them go.

Alec drug his feet in the dirt stirring up a little cloud of dust and hindering his swinging progress. "Are you breaking up with me?" he asked.

Emery laughed. "If it makes you feel better, I can call you up and nag you every once in a while."

"Well I suppose we can try it," Alec said as he started pumping his legs again.

They both half-heartedly swung for a while in companionable silence. Emery thought about how nice it was just being out here with him. She glanced over and noticed the serene look on his face as he watched the party in the distance.

The more she got to know him, the more she realized how much like his father he really was. Family was everything to Eric, and Alec was the same way. He was so excited to be an uncle again. Alec really was more than the charmer with a quick smile and a wink. Emery realized she might not know the half of it when it came to Alec.

"Oh!" Emery said. "I can't believe I haven't mentioned this to you. We found the photograph you sold to the old owners of our building—the arial that showed the entire town. It's breathtaking."

"Thanks," Alec said as he bit his lip. If the light were any better, she bet she would see him blush. "I got grounded for two weeks over that one. I climbed really high on the east side range and my parents were livid. I didn't mean to go that far by myself, but once I realized the shot if I just went a little higher, I kept going."

Emery stopped swinging and turned to the side, crisscrossing her chains. "You have a real gift Alec," she said sincerely.

Alec stopped and crossed his chains to so he could face her. "That's very nice of you to say."

"I mean it," she said. "I'd love to see more of your photography if you don't mind. I'd also love to feature some in the gallery once we get going."

"That's very sweet of you Emery, but I have no desire to get my pictures in a gallery," Alec said. "Maybe a long time ago I thought of things like that but not anymore."

Emery reached over and grabbed his chains where they crisscrossed and gave him a little shake. "This has nothing to do with being sweet and everything to do with me getting the best talent in the gallery."

Alec reached over and grabbed Emery's chains too, which pulled the two of them together. Emery's bare legs mingled with Alec's, sending tingles through her whole body. "I mean it, Em. Subject equals sore."

"All right," she said as her face was inches from his. "For now."

Emery always thought his eyes were just like Sugar and Violet's, but she noticed he had a small ring of light green around the pupil. She couldn't explain how he was looking at her—be it lovingly, lustfully, or tenderly, but however it was, it released bat-sized butterflies in her stomach.

Oh, this is a mistake, she thought as he closed the short distance between their lips. Her eyes fluttered shut as the excitement raced through her veins.

"OWWW," Alec said as he released Emery's swing. Emery heard the slap noise but didn't realize what it was until she saw Alec bend down and pick up the ball. The swing straightened out and she tried to get her raging hormones under control.

"Sorry, dude," a guy Emery didn't know said as he raced over to get the volleyball.

"Impeccable timing, Scott," Alec said with frustration as he lobbed the ball to the guy.

Emery stood up from the swing and straightened her skirt. "I think I need a refill," she said as Alec sighed and followed her back to the party.

Emery walked over to where Jackson stood at the

drink table, and he filled her glass back up with blackberry wine. "How's she doing," she asked Jackson with concern.

Sugar's pregnancy with Violet did not go well. She suffered from crippling morning sickness, and by the time she was recovering from that, her husband passed away. No, her memories from being pregnant with Violet were not good.

"She's doing great," Jackson said. "She told me about all the morning sickness with Violet, and she has none of that this time."

"He's going to be a hellion," Sugar interjected as she walked up with a big smile and slid her arm around Jackson's waist. "Violet was a god-awful pregnancy and she came out of the womb a thirty-five-year-old. This pregnancy is easy so he's going to be a handful once born."

Alec approached from one side and Madison and Hunter came from the other, and thankfully they seemed to let their feud have the night off.

"Well, it won't come from me—I was an angel," Jackson said.

Alec and Madison both burst out laughing at the same time. "Oh. My. God. Do you remember when you convinced us to set a trap for Santa? You were sure he'd come from up the hill behind The Lodge and we went out there with all those ropes and homemade booby traps?" Madison asked. "You both fell and hurt yourselves."

Alec snorted. "I had a broken arm and you jacked up your knee. Maddie had to run all the way home to get help or we would have frozen to death."

"Yeah, sure you were an angel, Jackson." Madison laughed and rolled her eyes.

Things became incredibly awkward when silence fell on the group and the twins both realized they were not only being decent to each other but were having a good time.

"Who wants some cake?" Sugar asked. "Hopefully not a lot of you because I feel like I could eat the whole thing. I'm starting to wonder if there are more than one in here," she said as she tapped her belly.

Emery stayed by the makeshift bar as everyone went their different ways. She needed a second to get herself together after that interlude with Alec. Emery seriously almost kissed him.

She hadn't missed the look on Madison's face when Alec called her Maddie. Emery thought she might tear up right then and there. Should she mind her business or help them? It hurt her heart to see this, but she didn't know what to do.

☙

Sugar, on the other hand, had no qualms about sticking her nose into this family feud. After everyone was gone Sugar, Jackson, and Emery picked up the random cups and plates that did not make it to the trash.

"We've got to be very careful about this," Sugar warned as Jackson took the bags of trash to the bear lockers. Bears hadn't been in the area in years, and they took great pains to keep it that way. "He's not having it at all. I've tried to get what I can out of him but he thinks we should let it go."

"How can we just let it go?" Emery asked as Sugar shrugged her shoulders. They entered the great room of the house from the back patio, and Emery immediately felt at home.

Sugar plopped down in a comfortable looking oversized brown chair and put her feet up. Emery was engulfed by the couch, its pillowy cushions comforting every muscle in her body. Two cats jumped up on Emery, and their large white Great Pyrenees, Thor, laid under Sugar's legs protectively.

The house was all open except for the bedrooms and bathrooms. The interior wood was bleached, and bamboo floors with different shades of brown were woven throughout.

Even from this vantage point Emery could see no expense was spared in the kitchen—it had a huge marble island almost as big as the one from the bakery. It was white with light-gray veins running through it. The cabinets were stained a distressed light blue, Sugar's favorite color.

"I don't know what's wrong with them," Sugar said. "It's a good thing they have us now. Oh shh, here he comes."

Jackson slid into the seat next to Sugar. "That's the last of it. You feel okay, Sug?"

Emery couldn't help but smile as Sugar assured him she was fine. She was so happy that Jackson had come into Sugar's life. After Josh, she feared Sugar would always be alone, too afraid to open up to someone else. She was well on her way to that kind of life until Jackson broke through her defenses.

"So, you and Alec looked cozy out there on the swings," Sugar said with a wide smile.

Traitor, Emery thought. Sugar was throwing her under the bus to get the conversation started.

"We were just talking," Emery said as she contemplated throwing a pillow at her. "Actually, I asked him about the photograph we found. I told him I'd love to display some of his work once the gallery is open, and he wanted no part of it."

Sugar grabbed Jackson's arm and put it around her, snuggling into him. "Why wouldn't he want his photographs shown? I'd think most people would be thrilled."

"That's a touchy subject for him," Jackson said. "He almost skipped a year of college when he was up for an internship with Miles Calhoun."

"Wow," Emery said. Miles Calhoun was a famous landscape photographer. "How did that happen?"

"It was an online contest. He had to send in his work and Miles narrowed it down to five people," Jackson explained. "Alec lost out at the very end."

Emery felt for Alec. That would be truly heartbreaking to get that close to working with someone so talented just to see it taken away.

"I don't see why that would stop him though," Emery said. "One disappointment shouldn't stop all that talent."

"At first it didn't," Jackson said, taking a sip of his beer. "When he came home the summer after his freshman year, he seemed to just give it up."

Sugar sat straight up and slapped Jackson on his chest. "The same time he started hating Madison!"

So much for being careful.

"All right, you two, I'm going to tell you all that I know and then we're going to drop it," Jackson said. "Remember I wasn't even here during all this—I was a little busy in Afghanistan," he said as Emery and Sugar nodded.

Jackson was two years older than the twins, and he joined the military after high school. A four-year contract was enough for him, especially with the action he saw in Afghanistan. Emery did not know the whole story, but she knew he still fought demons from that time.

"So, Alec came home for the summer with a renewed hatred of Madison. He messed up her relationship with her boyfriend as retaliation, and they have not gotten along since. That's all I know," he said. "By the time I got home a couple years later, this was all old news and no one wanted to bring it back up."

"Madison claims she has no idea why he started hating her so bad," Sugar said. "I bet the two are connected—his problem with Madison and the photography thing."

"Ok, no Lucy and Ethel business with this," Jackson said. "It's an old, deep wound and someone could get hurt."

"Someone is already hurt," Sugar pointed out. "Both of them."

"Do you think Madison would make up the fact that she didn't know why he hates her?" Emery asked. "Maybe if it were bad enough, she wouldn't want people to know."

"I don't think so," Jackson said. "Maddie and I have always been cool, even during her terrible high school years. She asked me one time if I knew why he hated her so much, and I don't think she was asking just for show."

With no more insight on the subject, the conversation wound down, and they parted ways to go to sleep. As Emery laid in the spare bedroom, she thought of how she almost kissed Alec that night and what an epic disaster that would have been. But Emery had come to care for Alec dearly, not just because he was her best friend's brother. Alec really was a great guy and Emery always relaxed and had fun around him.

Growing up she wanted something like Sugar and Jackson had found. It was practically predestined for the two of them to be together. From the minute they met there was a spark—an attraction that could not be denied.

Emery wondered if she'd ever have that as she cuddled into the snug bed. Growing up reading books like *Twilight* where true love was found instantly and happily ever after was assured, she couldn't help but want that for herself.

She was a grown up now and knew love at first sight didn't happen to everyone. Sometimes there was a slow burn leading up to love where a couple became friends and with mutual respect and understanding found love.

Even though she fiercely denied it to herself, she couldn't help but think of Alec as she drifted to sleep.

Chapter 5

"**WHAT DO YOU THINK, UNCLE ALEC?**" Violet asked as she held up a picture of mountains with a giant rainbow. She looked positively adorable in denim overalls with a pink t-shirt and matching pink boots.

"I think it's the best rainbow I've ever seen in my whole entire life!" Alec exclaimed as Violet broke into fits of giggles.

"Everyone, all your pictures are fantastic! There is no wrong in art." Alec walked around the room, inspecting everyone's pictures.

It was a rainy day and since most of the morning activities were cancelled, Alec set up a makeshift art room in the rec center for the children. The demographics for the hotel usually skewed young adult with no kids, but this summer they'd seen an uptick in families—this week in particular.

Thankfully, they saw this coming and purchased watercolor paints and crayons. Most of the parents were enjoying coffee on the covered porch or climbing the indoor wall while their children channeled their inner Picasso.

Sugar and Jackson were at their first prenatal appointment getting the first ultrasound. Violet, who loved hiking and climbing and all the things Alec was about chose to come stay with her Uncle Alec, not realizing things would be cancelled due to rain.

It did not matter. She was such an easy-going kid who loved to make pictures and she really loved her uncle. The children were all happily painting and the rain made an incredible sound on the metal roof. Staring out the window, Alec's eye caught a deer huddled under some nearby brush, and he wished he had his camera.

He could pull out his cell phone but it wouldn't do it justice. He would need to go out there and get as close as possible without startling the animal. But the room full of children couldn't be left alone, and he didn't have his camera.

There was a time when Alec was never without a camera. No matter where he went it, he had his trusty companion. Really Alec thought he put all this photography stuff to bed, but it was on his mind more and more frequently lately.

He didn't know if it was because of Emery bringing up that old photograph or because things were starting to run smoothly at the Snow Valley Hotel. The first couple of years were work, work, and more work as they got the new upstart up and running.

Determined to make it pay back the investment from The Lodge's coffers in first five years, Jackson and Alec took on many of the duties hotel employees would normally take care of. The open lot for RVs or tiny homes was a resounding success, and the hotel was at capacity.

Because of this, the hotel was operating in the black,

and they were able to hire more employees sooner than anticipated. Alec went from working eighteen-hour days to eight-hour days. Maybe that's why photography was back on his mind.

They owed a lot of this to Emery's hard work and his sister's support. Sugar promoted the hotel on several of her new cooking shows, and the numbers from social media and new reservations showed just how influential his half sister was.

Emery worked tirelessly getting their website and social media platforms updated. She taught them how to be consistent and keep people's attention. Not only did The Lodge, the Snow Valley Hotel, and Tiny House Park have their own social media outlets, but each of the owners also actually had their own.

Social media is currency, Emery would always say, usually when Alec appeared to be goofing off rather than setting his posting schedule. He must admit that dealing with Angela, the new social media manager for the company, did not carry the appeal of working with Emery and sucked the fun right out of it. He met her this week and gave her the schedule for the next two months. There was no need to hold back anymore.

As if thoughts could bring about reality, Emery appeared in the large rec room in another one of those sundresses that Alec loved. In the winter she was all preppy with her ever-present button-down Ralph Lauren shirts paired sometimes with a sweater, but these sundresses were starting to make Alec wish for eternal summer.

They had not spoken to each other since their near kiss at Sugar's party last weekend. He sure thought about it a lot. Emery kept herself busy during the rest of the party, and judging from her behavior, she'd consider it a big mistake to recreate the experience and take the near miss out of the equation.

Alec was starting to think that even if it was a mistake there was just no way they were going to avoid it happening. They were both reasonable grown adults. As long as the cards were on the table, he didn't see why two consenting adults couldn't enjoy each other for a limited time.

Emery was very pragmatic in her business dealings so he did not see how a slight flirtation between the two would be so tragic. Once it was over, they could go back to being friends instead of having all this tension all the time. If he were the paranoid kind, he'd think she'd been avoiding him since the party.

Deep down Alec knew you didn't just enjoy a hook up or two with a girl like Emery. First of all, he didn't think she'd be into that kind of situation, which is probably why she was avoiding him. Secondly, he didn't know if he could treat the situation as a hook up. Emery was the kind of girl you got serious with, and Alec had never done that.

He wasn't nearly as disciplined as Jackson when it came to making sure affairs were done well away from business, but he never led anyone on or told lies to get what he wanted. It would need to be a quick fling. Alec was never good at being Mr. Right, but he was excellent at being Mr. Right Now.

Come to think of it, he had not been Mr. Anything in quite some time. His workload was slowing down and it couldn't all fall on the fact that his wingman got married. No, something was afoot here.

Maybe it was seeing his father with Becca. When his parents divorced, he gave up on love just a bit. If his father could be so easily swayed with money to marry someone he didn't love, how valuable was love really?

Violet had deserted her rainbow and was talking animatedly with Emery, who knelt to her level. Emery's smile lit up her face and her eyes danced with a light Alec had never noticed before. She must have felt his stare because her gaze shifted to him and he felt like he was hit by a ton of bricks.

Oh no. No, just no. The pieces all just seemed to click together as she nodded her head in acknowledgement of him and continued her conversation with Violet.

Sexual attraction he could understand, but this feeling seeping through his heart was entirely unacceptable. *Get a grip*, he thought. The reason behind these unwelcome emotions was probably because she was off-limits. If he kept telling himself this, he might actually start believing it.

"Hi, Em," he said as he sauntered over. "Miss me already? Perhaps we can give Angela a different job here at the hotel."

Emery rolled those big gorgeous hazel eyes at him. "Angela is doing just fine," she said. "Sugar called and asked me to come over here. They are with your dad and Becca now."

Alec put his hands over Violet's ears. "Do you think everything is okay?" he asked with concern.

"I heard that," Violet said as she looked up at her uncle.

"I'm sure everything is fine," Emery said, pushing some of Violet's wayward hair behind her ear.

"Speak of the devil," Alec said when Jackson and Sugar entered the large room.

"Mommy, Daddy is everything okaaay," Violet asked as she ran toward her parents.

Jackson swooped her into his arms. "It's better than okay, sweetheart." He gave her a wink and a kiss on the cheek.

"Twins," Sugar said as she waved her arms skyward. "He knocked me up twice. Can you believe it?"

"What?" Alec and Emery exclaimed at the same time.

"Two babies?" Violet asked.

"Yes, two babies, monkey. You're going to have two brothers or sisters," Sugar answered as she put her arms around her husband and her little girl.

"I can't go to kindergarten next year, there's too much to do!" Violet exclaimed as everyone laughed.

Sugar and Jackson went to see Violet's picture, and Alec stopped Emery by gently taking her arm.

"Hey, do you still want to see some of my photographs?"

"What?" Emery asked, still dumbfounded by Sugar's announcement. "Oh yes, yes of course I do!"

Alec knew he was just looking for an excuse to keep her here but even as he realized it, he was incapable of stopping himself. He needed to explore these feelings and get it straightened out before he messed up everything.

œ

Emery sloshed through the path leading to Jackson and Alec's man cave. The rain was coming down in sheets now and Emery feared her umbrella wouldn't hold up. Lightening crackled across the sky and Alec and Emery picked up their pace.

Alec's abrupt about face confused her. Did he or did

he not want people seeing his art? They hadn't spent any time together since Sugar's party, and she wondered if it was a good idea to be alone with him in the middle of a storm.

It was too late to worry about that now as they reached the door to the large pole barn.

"This storm is crazy," Alec said once they were safely inside.

Emery shivered as the temperature dropped significantly with the growing storm. "I think walking from the hotel to here you've received as much rain as San Diego gets in a decade," Emery said.

Alec opened a closet door and grabbed a couple of hoodies. "Here you go," he said. "You look positively frozen."

Emery took the burgundy and blue Colorado Avalanche hoodie by its shoulders and held it out to give it a good look. The garment was at least three sizes bigger than she required.

"Not a fashion show, Em," Alec said as he slid his own hoodie on.

Oh, he's right, she thought as she pulled it over her head. Even with her height she realized this hoodie could double as a dress for her. But the chill started to melt away as Emery rolled up the long sleeves that went well past her hands.

"I'm going to start some coffee," Alec said as he went over to the small kitchenette. This place used to be a man cave—a place where Alec and Jackson could get away from their hotel. When rooms started filling up, Jackson and Alec needed to find alternative living conditions, and Jackson stayed here while Alec took the cabin in the woods.

Once Sugar and Jackson outgrew the apartment in the square, Alec agreed to switch with Jackson and moved into the makeshift man cave/apartment.

Emery had never visited a pole barn before, but she was pretty sure they weren't usually this nice. It was one big open room with two doors leading to two more rooms. The doors were open and Emery could see one was a bathroom, and the other was a bedroom.

Two massive recliners faced a huge television hung high on the wall. Beneath it were shelves that contained every video game Emery could name. Yes, this place was set up as a man cave on steroids.

A workbench stretched the length of one wall and it used to contain a bunch of Jackson's woodworking tools. The tools had moved to a small building by his new house, leaving it empty. Alec walked over and turned on the overhead lights.

He patted a stool signaling for Emery to sit down and went into the back bedroom. "I moved a lot of my old photos out here when I switched with Jackson," he said.

Poppy, the mother of Sugar's two cats jumped up on the workbench and stretched lazily in front of Emery. She smiled as she gave the cat a quick scratch behind her ears, and she was rewarded with a comforting purr.

"I see Poppy decided not to move," Emery said as Alec came back into the room, his arms stacked with photo albums higher than his head. She got up from her seat and took half the albums from him as he set the rest on the bench.

"Yes, she's not so much a house cat," Alec said. "She didn't do well over there—kept trying to escape. Now that she's back here she's perfectly content, aren't you

Poppy?" Poppy rubbed her face on the stack of albums and looked up adoringly at Alec as he gave her an affectionate pat.

Maybe it wasn't the house, Emery thought as Alec went back to the kitchen to grab the coffee, Poppy's eyes following him. Picking up an album from the pile, she began thumbing through it.

Blown away was an understatement. Emery looked inside a couple of the albums and realized they were sorted by season and composition. Never would Emery have thought that Alec could be this organized with anything.

Alec set a cup of coffee in front of Emery and she thanked him. As he pulled a stool up to the workbench she took a sip, and it was just how she liked it.

He didn't even ask how she took it, but he made it with very light sugar and very light cream. Emery racked her brain to come up with a time when she'd even had coffee with him.

"I haven't looked at these in forever," Alec said. Pulling a red album from the pile, he handed it to Emery. "These are all my favorites."

Each page displayed a photograph more impressive than the last. Emery stopped herself from removing some of them from their plastic protection just to look more closely. This album wasn't categorized like the others, and Emery had the feeling she was looking at Alec's greatest hits.

She turned to a page that wasn't a landscape, but an up-close portrait of an older woman. She looked regal, and the tilt of her head just said "try it buddy." A red beret and scarf accented her lovely skin, and her eyes were a beautiful shade of blue-green.

From other pictures around The Lodge, Emery knew this was the infamous Caitlin Larsson who was due to arrive this weekend, but she'd never seen her quite like this. This photo was almost challenging the viewer. No, that wasn't it. Caitlin was a survivor.

"This is unbelievable," Emery said, tapping the picture.

Alec smiled. "She hates it. Grandmother Caitlin would have my hide if she knew I still had this picture," he said sadly.

"Why?" Emery would be honored if someone took a photo of her like this.

"Who knows," Alec said. "She thought it made her look old or something." He went to turn the page but Emery stopped him.

"Look at her eyes," she said. "You've captured something so captivating and raw. It probably made her feel vulnerable."

Alec succeeded in turning the page this time. "Could be. All I know is I was told to destroy it, but I couldn't bring myself to do it."

"So I guess she won't be going up in the gallery?" Emery asked with a chuckle.

"Em, none of them are going up in your gallery." Alec sighed. "You wanted to see more, but I never said they could make their debut in your gallery."

Emery flipped to another page. "You are the most annoying human on the planet," she said matter-of-factly.

He chuckled as Emery held her hand to her chest. A teenage Madison sat on the windowsill of a large window. Emery had never seen this window at The Lodge, so it must have been from their childhood home. Her arms were wrapped around her knees and tears were leaking from her eyes, imitating the rain drops running down the window.

Her delicate elfin-like features brought an innocence to the picture that broke your heart.

"Alec," Emery said. "This picture is amazing. How can you keep them hidden away?"

"I forgot that was in there," Alec said. He got up from his stool to go refill his coffee. "I call it *The Devil Can Cry*."

With frustration seeping out of her pores, Emery continued to flip through the book. Every time she mentioned how good his photography was, Alec either told a joke or made a sarcastic comment. Emery never for one minute thought Alec was handed everything, but he did have it easy around this town. Even though she figured it annoyed him to some extent, she couldn't help but wonder if photography came easy to him so he took it for granted.

"Funny," she said. Once Alec sat back down, she looked him right in the eye. "Do you know what I would give to be talented like this? I've loved art my entire life and cannot make any of it."

"Em," Alec said softly. "You are the most talented person I know. The difference you made around here with social media? Picking just the right picture, putting up just the right posts. You've changed peoples' lives."

"Well, thank you." She felt her cheeks heat. "But that's not what I mean, and you know it."

"It's hard to explain," Alec said as he slid the stool back and began pacing. Emery couldn't help the small smile that sprang to her lips. Who knew pacing was a product of DNA? Sugar did the same thing when she needed to just get something out of her system.

"Photography was my world for a very long time," Alec said as he paced. "I really thought that would be my career. I even almost didn't go to college because of an internship that came up."

Emery wondered if she should bring up what she knew but decided to let him just talk. Sometimes people just needed to get things off their chest, and Emery had a feeling now was one of those times.

"It was with Miles Calhoun, who I just worshipped. He was having a contest for an assistant. It would be more like the guy going and getting his coffee, but to see him work! I was in the final five," he said. "Those pictures in that red album are what I sent in."

Emery tapped the book. "I'm surprised you didn't get it with these shots."

Alec stopped pacing and sat back down on the stool, turning it backward and leaning on the back. "What makes you think I didn't get it?"

"Jackson told us about it when Sugar and I were talking about your photography," Emery confessed guiltily. "We kind of badgered him into it. He never stood a chance."

Alec chuckled. "I can only imagine what the two of you can do when you get your minds together. It wasn't a secret, Em, but there is one that only two people know."

Emery held her breath as she waited for him to tell her, and he said nothing. "Alec, you can't say something like that and then not tell me what it is."

He bit his lip to keep the smile from forming. "Okay, okay. You win, although I have no reason why I'm going to tell you this," he said. "I actually won the contest."

"You did?" Emery asked utterly baffled. Her mind was

running with scenarios to explain why someone would turn that down.

"Yes, I did," Alec said. "But here's the kicker. I didn't find out that I won until a year later. Someone here intercepted the congratulations email and sent their own back turning down the position."

Emery's hand flew to her mouth. "Madison?"

"Ding, ding, ding," Alec said. "We have a winner. I ended up going to college at NYU, and at the end of freshman year we had a big party. The girl that I thought won was visiting a friend, and she came up to me and thanked me for not taking the job. When I looked at my email history, I found the email turning down the job, except I didn't write it."

Emery opened the album again and flipped through the beautiful photographs. The way he captured The Lodge, its property, and its inhabitants showed great care and a lot of love. It was a crime to keep this in the dark. Emery tried to rectify the Madison that she knew with a Madison who would do something like this.

"It doesn't make sense," Emery said as she closed the book. "Why would Madison do that?"

Alec shook his head. "I know you have this picture of Madison being this broken girl who just needed friends but, Em, it's not true. The real Madison hurts people like this."

"No, think about it, Alec. Really think about it. No matter what you feelings for her you must admit that she is a very smart woman. Madison has always wanted to run this place, yes?"

Alec nodded his head.

"If you won this internship, it would be a gift from

God," Emery explained. "You would be, pardon my pun, out of the picture. Even if she's as evil as you say, she wouldn't try and keep you from that."

Emery could see the doubt cloud over Alec's face. "Who knows why she does what she does," he said, even though Emery knew he didn't believe it. "Besides, when I opened the email, it had her damn signature at the very bottom. She must have had one of those auto-fill apps on her computer."

She knew this was going nowhere, but at least she knew why Alec held such ill will toward his twin. If it were true and Madison did that, she didn't blame him one bit.

"I'm assuming you never asked her about it, but since I know you aren't going to humor me, why don't you explain to me why you gave up photography?" Emery asked. "Obviously when you found out you won something so exclusive you must have realized how talented you are."

Alec picked up another photo album and began thumbing through it. "It was college really," he said. "I hated being away from here. Trust me, I'm glad I went, but after the disappointment of not getting it, then the realization that I did get it . . . combine all that with a good dose of homesickness and I decided that once I was finished with college, I would dedicate my life to The Lodge."

"That's a lot to unpack," Emery said, "but it doesn't mean you have to lock your camera away—your photographs away."

Alec sighed in frustration as he ran his fingers through his wavy blond hair. "I just didn't want to do something so important half-assed. I needed to focus on one thing and I decided The Lodge provided a more concrete future so I'd focus on that. That's why I don't show my pictures or sell them. What's the point?"

"The point is you're talented and this doesn't need to be an all or—"

"Okay, little miss do-gooder, that's enough for one day," Alec interrupted. "Better watch it or I might start trying to fix you."

"I'm not trying to fix you," she said with a playful slap to his arm.

"It sure seems that way," he said softly as he tilted on the stool and braced himself with his arm on the workbench so he wouldn't fall.

He was inches from Emery's mouth when all good sense left her and she closed the distance. The kiss was almost painfully sweet and soft until his other arm moved to the back of her head and he deepened it at an excruciating pace.

This was not what she expected a kiss from Alec would be like . . . not at all. She could tell he wanted to just go crazy, but he had an annoying amount of control. Just as she was about to start whimpering there was a loud knock at the door.

Alec pulled back and uttered a string of curse words that would even make Sugar blush. He sighed as Emery stood up quickly, practically knocking over her stool.

"Come in," Alec said between gritted teeth.

"Hey, can you come back?" Bob, one of the employees at the hotel asked. "The natives are getting restless and the rain has stopped. They're wondering if they can go on the hike now."

Emery grabbed her umbrella and scooped up her bag.

"I really need to get going anyway," she said. "I'm taking this and I'm telling Madison." She picked up the red album and tucked it under her arm.

"Em," Alec said, but she was already out the door.

Chapter 6

"**I MOST CERTAINLY DID NOT DO THAT,**" Madison said.

Emery and Sugar were over at The Lodge helping Madison with a couple of last-minute details for their grandmother's impending arrival and taste testing the desserts Sugar planned to make. Lounging on the grand patio outside the banquet room, Madison laid out in detail what she was preparing for the garden party when Emery hit her with the information she learned from Alec.

"Well that's why he was so mad at you," Sugar interjected. "If you had done it, I wouldn't blame him, but you two have been at each other's throats for nearly a decade for no reason."

Picking up her cup of tea, Emery swirled it around, looking at the dark liquid thoughtfully. It had been another busy week filled with learning and planning. Even though her kiss with Alec happened on Monday, here it was Thursday and she couldn't get it out of her head. Alec had texted her every day since their kiss, and she was trying to no avail to forget it ever happened.

At first he texted: "We good?" Emery assured him they were and to just forget it ever happened.

The next day, he texted: "What if I don't want to forget it ever happened?"

Emery realized forgetting about it wasn't going to be possible for either of them. The kiss sparked something between them that had been simmering beneath the surface, and it threatened to rage out of control.

"He'll never believe me," Madison said. "The stubborn a-hole will have to admit he was wrong, and that's not going to happen."

"We need to find out who did it," Emery said. "Who could it have been?"

Madison shrugged her shoulders. "I mean, if it was through email, anyone could have done it. Alec is the worst at making up passwords, especially back then. It was always our current dog's name. Anyone with a grudge against him could have done it."

Sugar popped one of the individual tarte tatin's in her mouth and sighed. "These are delicious, if I do say so myself," she said. "Did anyone have a grudge against Alec? I mean, it seems like everyone in this town worships him."

"Don't remind me," Madison said as she followed suit and tried the tarte tatin. "My god, that's good. Someone must have used my computer at The Lodge. I had a program that automatically attached my signature file to any outgoing emails. My Dad made me take it off the computer when it attached my email signature to an important email he sent out. I was working in the front desk area; anyone could have used it."

"What about a girlfriend?" Sugar pondered. "Maybe there was someone who didn't want him away from home."

"That could be," Madison said. "Our dear brother

wasn't always the sharpest tool in the shed when it came to women. I know in his late teens dad had to have a talk with him about *'dating'* the customers or our employees."

"What about someone who didn't want him to skip college," Emery said thoughtfully as she took a bite of a small croissant filled with chicken salad. She didn't want to hear about Alec's past dalliances. "These are a keeper," she said, pointing to the pastry.

"I'm sure my parents weren't thrilled, but they were supportive," Madison said. "My grandmother was furious, but she can't work her cell phone, much less hack Alec's email.

Sugar stretched her long arms above her head. "How long ago did she move away?"

Emery knew Sugar's grandmother was a sensitive topic and she worried about the upcoming visit. Sugar was upset that the woman had hurt her father by not attending his wedding. She had to feel rejected by the woman, which was one of Sugar's fears when she wanted to look for her father. Sugar had problems with impulse control, and that became heightened with strong emotions. It was a dangerous mix.

"When my parents first divorced, my mom didn't come out. It wasn't until the woman I grew up knowing as Aunt Mary became my mom's wife that grandmother had issues," Madison said. "She packed up her things and moved to Florida with her sister, claiming she couldn't take another Colorado winter."

"But winter is the only time she visits," Sugar pointed out.

"Of course. She left because my father wouldn't let her dump all over my mom," Madison said. "The structure of this whole business skews toward the males. Grandmother has a nice salary coming from this place, but absolutely no say-so in anything."

"That's jacked up," Sugar said. "Dad's changed that now, though, right?"

"Yes, but don't be surprised if she's not super friendly with your mom. She's just another in a long tradition of women who think their son is perfect," Madison said. "Just like Alec can never do anything wrong."

Emery came from a long line of strong women and couldn't imagine what Madison had gone through growing up in this kind of environment. Emery's mother may not be the most maternal person in the world and may have problems expressing her emotions, but she dang sure supported her daughter and encouraged her to follow her dreams.

For the first time since stepping foot in Snow Valley, Emery thought Sugar was better off not growing up here, and maybe she shouldn't be so envious of other people's families just because they were different than her own.

"At least you and Alec can get things straightened out now," Sugar said.

Madison took a sip of her tea and appeared to be in deep thought. "Why would I want to do that? He was the jury and judge on this case and gave me a sentence that ended with my heart being broken in a million pieces. So he can believe what he wants."

Nothing would get settled here today, but Emery was happy they seemed to get to the bottom of the little family feud. She knew Madison was right about one thing—unless they found out who actually did it, Alec would never believe Madison when she said she didn't.

Madison's phone vibrated and she pushed her chair back. "I need to take this," she said as she walked to the other side of the patio, talking business.

"I don't think there's much more we can do," Emery said. "But at least we know what it was and that Madison didn't do it."

"Oh, there's a lot more we can do," Sugar said.

"Sug—

"What? I'm the baby sister. I have a lot of years to make up. I'm going to tell on them to our parents," she said, smiling proudly.

Emery's eyes grew round and wide. "You wouldn't."

"Watch me, Em. Just watch me. This family is going to be whole again before these dudes are born," she said as she patted her tummy.

"You seem awful certain they are boys," Emery said. "Are you sure you want to just flat out tell on them?"

"I was sure they were twins too and look how that turned out," she said with a wink. "I can just tell, and my boys are going to have an aunt and uncle who at least can bear to be in the same room with each other."

ॐ

Emery was delighted with how the interior of the gallery was proceeding so quickly. Her heeled sandals clicked on the red brick as she walked along the square, heading toward the town hall. She took a big breath of fresh air and said her good mornings to people she passed on the sidewalk.

The square was abuzz with people shopping, dining, or just out to have a good time. The word was spreading about this place, and just yesterday, one of the pop stars who stayed in one of the private mansions came out to get a pastry from Sugar's bakery and stayed to watch the movie in the square.

You can't buy that kind of publicity. The wholesome environment was incredibly charming, and it seemed to suit both the luxury guests and the more modest guests that stayed at the Snow Valley Hotel. Never in Emery's wildest dreams did she think all the work they did would be this successful.

All the work she'd done was paying off in spades. Today was their weekly farmers market, and the giant square had booths filled with fresh vegetables and artisan products. She made a mental note to visit Franny's stand when she finished with the mayor. That woman made the cutest hats, gloves, and mittens. It might be summer now, but Emery knew winter came knocking early around here.

Would she still need to be here then? she thought. The Lodge and its properties were completely independent now. Most of the businesses in the square jumped on the social media bandwagon quickly when the Snow Globe Café took off. Now she just needed to turn in these permits for the new gallery and check on the town's new website/social media manager.

There was still the issue of the gallery. Emery had to admit it—Sugar was right. It's funny how those dreams you have when you're a child get pushed to the background once you become an adult. SJL would always be her pride and joy, but the gallery fed her very soul.

For Emery, the lure of discovering new talent spoke to her more than anything. So many great artists are never seen because they aren't in the right place or just don't know how to get their art seen.

Emery's *plans* had plans for this. It would involve a lot of travel, but Emery loved traveling. Perhaps Snow Valley would become her home base. More and more she was beginning to think that logically it was the best decision.

With Sugar's news, it about cinched it. Did she want to miss a minute of those twins growing up? She'd gone back to San Diego for three short months and it felt like Violet went from a toddler to a child. Sugar would need help too, and Emery already knew Sugar would never hire a nanny, not in a million years.

Reaching the corner building opposite the gallery, Emery opened the door and went inside the bustling county seat. Not only did it house the town hall, but the police department was also there.

"Emery!" the town's mayor Grant greeted her warmly. He enthusiastically shook her hand. Nearing his seventies, Grant was a sweet elderly gentleman with bright, happy eyes and a slight potbelly. "Do you have the paperwork?"

"Right here," Emery said as she handed him the documents. She needed a few permits for holding events in the new space and some electrical upgrades for the new artist studio going in the old storage area.

"Don't you worry about a thing, we'll push these right though," he said kindly. Emery didn't know if it was the work she did for the town or her association with the Larsson clan, but things happened very quickly for her around here.

It didn't sit right with her. "No really, Mayor, that's fine. It'll be a few months before we'll even need these."

"That's our Emery," Grant said. "Always prepared!"

She smiled and said her goodbyes and couldn't help the warmth she felt when he said "our Emery." It was nice to be part of a community, and this community had welcomed her with open arms.

Emery watched television shows and movies about small towns, but had never experienced it for herself. It was shocking that they accepted her, and a tiny part of her knew she was shocked because of her mixed heritage.

Another gift Emery received from her first boyfriend Quentin. Sugar was right—she did have issues from her relationship with him. Her issues had issues.

"Emery!" Mrs. Eskildsen called from across the busy room, waving her arms. Mrs. Eskildsen owned a small nail salon on the square. A widow for ten years, she was seventy-five years young and full of energy.

She made her way to Mrs. Eskildsen who engulfed Emery in a big hug.

"Well that was a wonderful greeting," Emery said as she smiled her. "What did I do to deserve such a wonderful hug, Mrs. Eskildsen?"

"Doris, call me Doris," Doris Eskildsen scolded. She'd told Emery on more than one occasion to call her Doris. "Why just for being you! Do you know what happened yesterday?"

"No, what happened yesterday?" Emery curiously asked.

"That singer, the one all the kids love? Her real name is Katie but she goes by some weird name. Well, she came to my shop and got a manicure yesterday! We talked and laughed, and she posted a pic on Instagram of the two of us!"

"That's wonderful," Emery said. "Do you know what that'll do for your business?"

Doris laughed. "Thanks to you I do! My little shop has over 200,000 followers now! I didn't even have Instagram before you. Heck, I didn't even have a smart phone!"

Doris hugged Emery again. "That's not even the best part. My grandkids in Chicago, well let's just say they think they have the hippest, coolest grandmother ever now! You are a blessing, a true blessing to this town Emery Cooper."

She gave Emery's cheek a pinch and was on her way. Emery felt a warmth spread through her body as she hugged herself. This was the reason why she took the chamber of commerce on as a client. She knew Sugar would drive people to the town, and she wanted these small mom and pop shops to benefit. Seeing it come to fruition just made Emery's soul happy.

As she was about to exit, Emery saw Matt through the glass door that led to the police station. He noticed her and sent her a wave. Emery opened the glass door and head in.

"Hi, Matt," she said, walking up to him.

Matt smiled at her as he set his clipboard down. "Emery, it's good to see you! You aren't here for anything official I hope," he said with a smile.

"No, no I was just passing by and saw you and thought I'd say hello."

"Emery!" Chief Barker exclaimed. "How are you? You aren't here for anything official I hope."

Emery and Matt laughed in unison. "It's kind of the standard joke around here if you couldn't tell," Matt said.

Chief Barker, otherwise known as Gina's stepdad,

tapped on Matt's clipboard. "I need that report within the hour," he said.

"Now, Emery, I hear you might be starting a residency for artists. My daughter is an artist back in New York," he said. "Would you like to see some of her work?"

"Sure," Emery said. She gave Matt a smile as Chief led her to his office. Word sure spread fast in a small town.

Gina wasn't around, but her stepdad sure filled in for her just fine.

○✼

"Sug, I tell you, her sculpting and pottery are amazing," Emery said. It had been a full day since her run in with the Chief, and Emery still couldn't stop thinking about his daughter's work.

Emery was at the café helping Sugar with the finger foods and desserts for the garden party tomorrow. Taste testing was considered helping too, and Emery was up for the job.

"Really? That's great. Jackson is good friends with her brother, Jack. He's the local conservation officer and moonlights at his grandparents' Christmas tree farm," Sugar said. "The one where Jackson took Violet and I last year."

"Hmm," Emery said, licking the peach preserves off her fingers. "I wonder how she ended up in New York and her whole family is here?"

With excellent proficiency, Sugar picked up another macaron and expertly filled it with frosting. "From what I know, Chief and his first wife moved to New York City when they were young, and after she passed, Chief and Jack moved back here."

When Emery first entered the chief's office, she really did not know what she was about to see. At first, she was being polite. Emery assumed that once the word was out, many people would want her to look at their family or friend's art. In a small town it didn't take long for the word to spread everywhere.

The first thing that caught her eye was his coffee cup. It was gorgeous and hand carved with mountains and trees with gradient colors from pink at the top to dark brown on the bottom. Right away Emery knew Angelica, Chief Barker's daughter, was immensely talented. After going through pictures on her website, Emery did not think she was the best fit for the opening, but she'd be a perfect candidate for a residency here at the gallery.

Basically, the residency would cover the artist's basic expenses—food, lodging, and art supplies. It would give them the chance to focus solely on their art and creativity. Emery was converting the old stockroom into an artist studio, and at the end of the residency they would have an opening of the artist's work.

She was looking into ordering a few kilns and had already booked an electrician to upgrade the electricity. With Becca's generous offer, she could afford to put a whole potter's studio in, and maybe some glass furnaces.

"I think she's a great candidate for our first residency," Emery said. Initially, Emery wasn't sure how they'd go about picking an artist for the residency, so Angelica would make a great first choice until the program was completely ready. After that, the artist would have a choice of a six-month or yearlong residency, and maybe Angelica would love to spend the time with her family.

"Sounds good," Sugar said. "Hey, can you pack up the croissants? I'm running out of room."

The large marble worktable was filled with Sugar's delectable desserts. Shrimp cucumber canapes, chocolate hazelnut scones, lemon bars, and macarons in every color of the rainbow filled most of the surface. Grabbing one of the Sugar Jones boxes, Emery expertly put it together and began stacking desserts.

"So, what are you going to do with the two apartments above the building expansion," Emery asked.

There were three buildings in total. The café was the third building from the corner of the square, and Sugar had bought the first buildings—the one on the corner and the one in between. Excluding the corner building where the art gallery would be, Sugar would be able to triple her eating area in the café.

"I hate to turn them into something else. Housing is hard to find close to the square. Maybe we can use one of those apartments for your residency," Sugar offered.

If Emery didn't need her second apartment above the gallery for the artist in residence, she had a different idea for it.

"Sug, that would be amazing!" Emery said. "I've been thinking. When the renter in the second apartment above the gallery moves out, I might move in there."

"Because you're moving here?" Sugar said with that big movie star smile of hers.

"Don't get too excited, Sugar," Emery warned. "Trial basis."

Sugar moved on to making those tiny chicken salad croissants that Emery loved so. "I'll take what I can get. It's perfect, and you can stay in the apartment above here as long as you want. I'm never changing it, especially with these two on the way. I think we may end up staying here half the time once they're born."

It really was perfect. Besides a few design changes, living on the square was a great solution. Emery loved nature, but she had no desire to live in the woods where bear lockers were necessary. Also, the apartment was larger than her condominium back in San Diego, so she knew all her things would fit.

The current renters planned to move out that fall, but maybe Emery could make them an offer they could not refuse. Now that she said it out loud, she was excited about all the possibilities.

The only thing she would need to do was tell her parents, and that part was not exciting.

"Are you sure you won't come to breakfast tomorrow?" Sugar asked. The family was having a welcome breakfast for Caitlin ahead of the garden party.

"No, Sug, that's a family thing," Emery protested.

"You are just as much family to me as they are and you know it," Sugar said stubbornly.

Emery opened another box and moved on to the macarons. "I'll be at the garden party, but I think I'll take a pass on being family with your grandmother," she teased.

"Thanks. Some best friend you are!" Sugar said. "Em, I don't know how I'm going to do this. I don't know how I can be decent to this hateful woman."

Emery walked over and put her arm around Sugar's shoulders. "You are going to be just fine," she said. "Besides, if anything happens, blame it on pregnancy hormones."

Sugar laughed. "I need that excuse for something else,"

she said with a triumphant grin. "I ratted out Madison and Alec to my mom and dad today."

After a quick intake of breath, Madison whispered, "You didn't."

"I did!"

Oh boy, Emery thought.

○₹

Alec hurried along the path going to the main house. His mother called him and said she urgently needed to talk to him. Fear spiked his adrenaline as he took the large porch stairs three at a time.

Grandma Caitlin flew in earlier this afternoon, but his dad took her straight to her room at The Lodge. She refused to stay in the main house now that his mother and her wife, Mary, lived there and said she wouldn't be comfortable out in the middle of the woods with Eric and Becca.

In typical Caitlin fashion, she needed to have her beauty rest before she saw anyone, so he wouldn't see her until tomorrow morning. Travel time always included recuperating for Caitlin, even if she hadn't seen her grandchildren in over a year. Alec now wondered if there was something wrong with her health.

He rushed into the big formal living room and stopped dead in his tracks when he saw the long table. His father, Eric, and mother, Allison, sat in the middle, flanked by their respective partners, Becca and Mary. Madison sat across from them, her hands folded on the table, gazing at them with mild disinterest.

One thing was for sure, his sister always did have the

best poker face in the tri-town area. Alec was sure guilt read across his face, and he didn't even know what he did.

"Come in, Alec," Allison said. "Take a seat next to your sister."

Alec took a deep breath and sat down. He didn't sit next to Madison exactly, but left one seat open between them, causing his mother to lift an eyebrow.

"What'd we do now?" Alec asked, wanting to get the show on the road. However, the pit in his stomach told him he would not like whatever they had to say. He wasn't going to like it at all.

"Your sister came to see us all this morning," Eric stated.

Alec shook his head. He knew what this was about. Emery told Sugar, who then in turn told the parents. Sugar was what, twenty-six years old? He did not need this level of meddling in his life.

"We know everything—we know about your photography internship and what happened, and we know about what happened with Rick."

The familiar sense of guilt he felt whenever Rick was discussed bubbled in Alec's chest. He was Madison's first real boyfriend. Rick was a great guy, and when everyone started talking about their past, he shared that he was bullied as a kid. Still stung from Madison destroying his internship, he told Rick about Madison's past behavior and gave him receipts to prove it, ruining their relationship.

Even though part of him felt justified doing it, a bigger part of him was appalled that he had become that kind of person. He swore after he did it, he would never be vengeful and hateful again.

This little intervention might test his resolve, and baby sis might need to look out.

"Madison, I'm only going to ask you this one time," Eric said. "Did you intercept Alec's acceptance email and write one back turning it down?"

"I most certainly did not," Madison said, her chin held high as she looked her father right in the eye.

Alec snorted.

She turned in her chair to face him. "I did not do it, but you did take Rick to the side and explain my high school behavior, didn't you?"

"Yes," he said, feeling that guilt again.

"Then there's really nothing else to say," Madison said, facing the parents again. "He'll never believe me and I will never trust him. Are we done here?"

"Your email signature was at the bottom of the email," Alec said.

"Well, if someone used my computer at front desk then it would auto attach it. Maybe one of your little *friends* did it after they found out you didn't want to be their boyfriend," Madison said.

That pit was back in his stomach and he had the feeling that he'd been terribly wrong all these years. He just couldn't bring himself to admit it.

"No, we are not done here, Madison," Eric said sternly. "We are a family. It's time for this nonsense to stop."

"Violet asked me the other day why you two hate each other," Becca said quietly.

Becca might as well have gotten up, walked over to him, and smacked him across the face. Looking over at Madison, he saw her chin quiver slightly but then she regained control.

Madison cleared her throat. "I'm sorry Violet has been affected," she said. "I'm sure Alec agrees that we'd never want to cause her any pain and will try to behave better when she's around."

Alec just nodded his head yes, not trusting his voice. It was just like when they were little and in trouble. Madison was always the peacemaker and knew how to get them out of trouble, and Alec just sat there and agreed.

"If that's all we're going to get then it's a step in the right direction," Allison said.

Madison scooted her chair back and stood up. "Good, now if we are done, I need to get to the café to pick up the food Sugar prepared ahead for tomorrow."

Alec knew damn well that Sugar was bringing those desserts to The Lodge on her way home. Madison was going over there to tell her off. *Not without me*, he thought as he said his goodbyes and raced to his truck.

Chapter 7

ALEC WAS PULLING UP just as Madison started banging on the back door to the café. "Sugar, open this door right now!" she yelled.

Wow. Madison usually kept her emotions on an even keel. She was angrier than he was. He got out of his own car and made it to the doorway just as Emery opened the door. Madison shot around her, and Emery looked like she was going to make an escape.

He braced his arm on the other side of the door. "Where do you think you're going?"

"Uhh, this seems like a sibling thing," she said.

"Emery, get your ass back here," Madison called.

His anger almost dissipated at the look of fear on Emery's face. She turned around and headed back into the bakery.

"You had no right," Madison was half yelling at Sugar. "Why would you do that?"

"Yeah," Alec said. "Telling our parents at our age?"

"Well, you gave me no choice and I have a medical condition," she said as she stared them both down defiantly, her hands on her hips.

"What medical condition?" Alec asked as he opened one of the boxes and popped a canape in his mouth.

Sugar smacked at his hands. "Those are for tomorrow."

"Aww, will you have to make them again if we eat them?" Madison asked as she slid next to Alec and ate a canape.

"Cut it out," she said. "You know I have ADHD and poor impulse control. I can't help myself sometimes."

Alec snorted. "So your ADHD, which causes you not to be able to concentrate well, caused you to drive to The Lodge property, find all our parents, assemble them, and tell them what you know about us."

"That sounds about right," Sugar said. Madison picked up another canape. "I said stop it."

"You can't just come in here and cause problems, Sugar," Madison said. "This isn't some game."

"I think we all need to calm down," Emery said holding her hands out.

"Spoken like someone who started it all," Alec seethed.

"Don't you talk to her like that," Sugar said.

"It's okay, Sug," Emery said. "I told you I was going to tell. This isn't new."

Madison let out a breath. "I told you flat out he'll always hate me. It doesn't matter."

"It does," Sugar said, tears beginning to well up in her eyes.

Alec, panicking because Sugar was about to burst into tears, tried to deflect the situation. "See, I don't hate her," he said as he put his arm around her.

"Don't touch me," Madison said, shoving him off.

He stood there for a split second, and just like when they were little kids, he couldn't resist and reached out, touching her forearm with the tip of his index finger.

"I'm going to kick your ass," Madison yelled as Alec started backing up.

"Not fair, I can't hit you back!"

Alec kept walking backward until he hit his head on some hanging pans. There was nowhere else for him to go.

"I believe you, all right. Are you happy now?"

"What did you say?" Madison asked.

"I believe you, that you didn't do it," he said softly. "I was wrong for blaming you without even asking. There was just no one else who would want to do that to me."

Exasperated, Madison threw up her arms. "Why would you think I'd want to do that to you? I know I could be a grade A jerk for a while there, but I never did anything to you. You're my brother."

Alec watched Emery go put her arm around a sobbing Sugar.

"I figured you found out I was the one that gave Dad your Facebook attacks in high school."

"That was you?" she exclaimed with wide eyes. "I never knew you did that, and if I did, I would have thanked you. I did not want to be that person. I only acted that way because I was terrified people would do it to me."

She was happy about this? "Why would you thank me? You were in so much trouble over that."

Madison punched him in the arm. "Because it was an out. My parents found out so I couldn't participate anymore, not because I was weak. You really know nothing about being a teenage girl, do you?"

Alec swallowed hard. "I'm sorry I told Rick about you,"

he said. "I had no right, even if it were you who turned down my internship. I still shouldn't have done it and I've felt bad since the words left my mouth."

Madison drew in a deep breath and let it out. "It was probably for the best. I knew his history so I hid mine. He never would have dated me if he knew I was a former bully, so I hid it. We would have just gotten more attached and it would have hurt even worse if it went on longer, so I forgive you."

Alec didn't know what to say and just stood there in shocked silence. Madison sighed and started to turn away. He closed the distance between them with his long legs and picked her up off the ground into a massive bear hug.

"OMG, Alec, put me down!" Madison said as she swatted at his back. "You know I hate being treated like a little kid."

"Who made my wife cry," a menacing voice said. Alec put Madison down and they faced a terribly upset Jackson.

"They made up and Emery's moving here!" Sugar said between sobs as she wrapped her arms around her husband and cried in earnest into his chest.

Jackson looked at Emery helplessly.

"Welcome to the first trimester," Emery said with a smile. "It gets better, I promise."

○₹

Emery practically skipped back to her building. Finally, the twins' problems were ironed out, and she got away without talking to Alec about their kiss. She wanted to check on a few more things at the new gallery before turning in for the night.

Unlocking the front door, she entered and turned on the lights. Individual overhead lights on each wall came to life, with larger lights hanging in the middle of the room. Lighting was everything for an art gallery, and thankfully the novelty store lit the space well.

She would just need a few more spotlights installed in the middle of the room. Looking at both sides she realized she would need more lighting there too. Opening her phone she jotted down a note to have the electrician look into wiring more lights on the sides. By the time this was complete, that electrician was going to be Emery's new best friend.

Emery decided on a gorgeous chocolate brown for the floors. Everything else was already white, which was perfect because she didn't need anything to distract from the art. A contractor had her penciled in for next week to start on the floors, and she was happy with that.

The wall between the corner building and its neighbor now had an outline, which would become two pocket doors. They would remain locked unless there was an event, at which point they would open to reveal an area where people could talk and eat and drink.

She rolled one of the walls on wheels. A local builder made a test wall using Emery's version. It would be a bit like playing Jenga. She could arrange the room any way she wanted. The wheels had locks, so she simply locked them once they were in their rightful place. Emery studied the wall and decided she needed a few different heights to make the room more dramatic.

Emery's phone vibrated in her pocket. "Hi, Mom,"

she said as she answered her mother's FaceTime request. This wasn't their regularly scheduled day, so Emery hoped nothing was wrong.

From the look of her screen, Laura Cooper was going out that night. Emery could see the top of her strapless, red beaded dress. Her braided hair was pulled together into a bun and she looked radiant. A richer shade of mocha than Emery, she looked like an African Queen.

"Emery, how is everything?" her mom asked.

"Going great, how about you? You look fantastic," Emery said with a smile.

"This old thing?" Laura asked with a laugh. "Your father and I are going to a premier tonight, and as usual, he's taking forever to get ready."

For years it was a running joke that in the getting ready department, they switched bodies. As organized and focused as Emery, Laura was always prepared while her father floundered because he was distracted by something else.

Her parents always made quite a look together. Her father was tall and blond and would blend perfectly in Snow Valley, where a significant portion of the population hailed from a Norwegian country. Laura's mother was also tall, but her mother was Mexican and her father was African American. Laura was the spitting image of her mother, but her skin was darker and her hair curlier.

"Are you in the gallery?" Laura asked.

Emery took some time showing her mother the lighting and the walls with her camera. Technology really did help you stay close to people when there was a distance between you.

"Well, the reason I called is to ask when you are

going to have the opening with Becca's illustrations," her mother asked. "The word has leaked out, and people are driving me crazy wanting tickets."

Emery would bet that word leaked right out of Laura Cooper's mouth. She didn't blame her. If she were Becca's agent, she would do the same thing.

"There's still a bit to go, so not at least until early fall," Emery said. "Don't worry, you'll be the first one to get tickets, especially after you gave Becca the idea."

"Ah, she told you about that, did she?" A smile broke out over her face.

"Yes, she did. I was surprised," Emery said.

Laura furrowed her brow. "Emery Louise Cooper, why would that surprise you?"

Not trusting her voice, Emery shrugged her shoulders.

"I'm very proud of you, Emery," Laura said. "Don't you ever doubt that for a minute. I'm busy and sometimes I don't take the time to say these things, but that's my fault, you hear me?"

"I forgot to show you the lighting in the middle," Emery said as she focused the camera toward the ceiling. "Yes, I hear you. Thank you, Mama," she said wiping her tears quickly while the camera was pointed away.

"Anyway, have you decided on a name?"

Focusing the camera on herself once more, Emery laughed. "If only. Sugar and Violet voted to call it Emery Cooper."

"I'd vote for that too," her dad said as he came into focus next to her mother. "Perfect name."

"I don't know. Sugar says since the other side of the business has her name this side should have mine." Emery said. "I need to think about it."

"Well, once you have it, let me know. Do you know August Rainer?" her mother asked.

"Of course I do!" Emery exclaimed. "He has an art blog that's been featured in *Vogue*. Everyone reads him."

"Well, he was one of the people that contacted me and wants to do an interview about the new gallery and why it's located in Snow Valley," her mom explained.

Emery was genuinely gobsmacked.

"I'll take your silence to mean you're interested," her mom joked.

She nodded her head enthusiastically and took a deep breath. "Since you're both here, I want to tell you something. I'm going to do a trial move out here. I don't have my condo in San Diego anymore and this town just suits me."

"That's wonderful," her mom said as her dad nodded in agreement.

"You aren't mad or upset?" Emery asked. "All your kids have moved away."

"Oh, sweetheart, it isn't like we wouldn't love to have you right here," her mom said. "When you raise children, you hope they'll find their own path, their own happiness. Hopefully you've found yours now."

"Besides, since Becca is out there with you, we have a feeling we'll be in Snow Valley quite a bit in the future," her dad, Avery, said. Becca was their biggest client and they had all become family over the years.

Emery didn't doubt that they'd be coming to town somewhat regularly. The Coopers and the Jones had celebrated holidays together since Emery was in third grade. Her parents came out for Christmas and Easter this year. There was no reason why they shouldn't continue with that, and they loved the luxury of The Lodge.

Emery took a deep breath after they ended their FaceTime. That was easier than she thought it would be. Why was it so hard for people to just get out of their own heads and talk about things? Between a decade-old fight and Emery being scared to tell her parents she was moving, so much emotion was wasted over nothing.

Her phone vibrated again when a text came through: "So you're moving here. My kiss must have been awesome."

Emery's mouth dropped in outrage and she shot him a reply: "I'm moving here on a trial basis."

She tapped her long French-manicured nails on her phone. *Oh, what the hell*, she thought.

Before she could overthink it, she typed: "Your kiss was more than awesome."

○₹

Alec whistled as he made his way to the main house for breakfast with his grandmother. He was still in a good mood from Emery's text last night. Wearing a white polo and tan chinos with docksiders, he knew his grandmother would be pleased. As he neared the house he saw Sugar, Jackson, and Violet coming from the other direction.

Sugar looked completely hostile wearing her beautiful rose-colored sundress. Jackson also wore a polo shirt in blue with khaki pants. Little Violet was adorable as ever in a little sundress covered with her favorite flower—violets.

"Why do we have to get dressed up for breakfast," Sugar complained as they came within earshot.

Madison pulled up in her golf cart. Alec never blamed her for riding that golf cart everywhere. How she managed to walk at all in those sky-high heels she wore all the time was a mystery to him.

"Because dear, sweet Caitlin may have left Connecticut for this baren wasteland of culture, but we don't have to act like we are heathens," Madison explained.

"Great," Sugar said as she looked at Jackson.

"It's going to be fine," he said.

"Hey," Madison said.

"Hey." Alec put his hands in his pockets and averted his gaze.

Well, this was awkward. How do you start talking to someone you have immensely disliked for a long time? He went from Madison being the devil to him being the real villain of the piece. It would just take some time.

They all entered the great big dining room again to find Caitlin poised as ever, speaking with Becca and Eric. Alec looked around but didn't see his mother or Mary.

Madison leaned closer. "Grandmother didn't want Mom or Aunt Mary here," she whispered.

"It's their house," Alec cried. Madison just shrugged her shoulders.

"And this must be Sugar," Caitlin said as she got up to greet her. Alec noticed it seemed difficult for her to stand up, which was not the grandmother he knew.

While she may be stiff and formal, his grandmother was a bundle of energy, always buzzing here and there. In fact, she looked frail and like she had aged ten years instead of the year and a half she'd been gone.

She still looked impeccable, even if her clothes

looked a tab bit big for her. Caitlin always had her clothes tailored to fit, so she must have recently lost some weight. Her white silk button-down shirt hung just a little loose, and her gauzy lilac skirt was a little big around the waist.

"Hello," Sugar said as Caitlin gave her a hug and kissed both cheeks.

"My goodness, your grandfather would have been beside himself if he'd had the chance to meet you," Caitlin said. "You look so much like her."

Alec knew he was talking about his grandfather's mother. He loved his mother fiercely, and Sugar was her spitting image.

"Jackson," she said stiffly as she kissed both his cheeks. The elder Larssons constantly feuded with Jackson's father, Paul.

"It's good to see you, Caitlin," Jackson answered back.

"And you must be Violet," Caitlin said as she took her hands.

"I'm Violet Jones Anderson, and I'm pleased to meet you grandma," she said.

"What a wonderful little girl!" Caitlin exclaimed. "Such good manners!"

After the introductions were over and the food was served, everyone seemed to relax.

"You're doing good," Alec said softly to Sugar. "I don't think she's well," he added.

Sugar shook her head in acknowledgment as she cut her delicious stuffed French toast.

"So, Alec, tell me about this new hotel," she said. "It's called the Snow Hotel or something?"

Alec set his fork down and took a nice sip of coffee.

"Snow Valley Hotel, and it's doing wonderful. Jackson and I are operating in the black already."

"That's nice, dear," she said as she pushed the food around on her plate. "I'm still not sure why it was needed when so much else is going on here."

Eric sighed. "Diversifying our client base is always a good idea. Father showed us that when he built the cabins. Besides, if we didn't open another hotel, I feared Madison and Alec would kill each other."

"That's nonsense. They just had a little friendly competition going on," she said, patting Madison's hand. "It's good for the soul."

"No, mother, it wasn't. Alec thought Madison cheated him out of an opportunity and they've barely been able to speak to each other since."

Caitlin laughed. "Are you talking about that photography job after high school?" she inquired. "Don't be silly, I had one of the front desk men take care of that."

Silverware clanked as they fell from shocked hands to their plates.

"How could you?" Alec asked.

"How could I not, dear boy? Do you think for a minute I'd let you run away from here without going to college? To be a photographer?" Caitlin said. "You have responsibilities to this family and this business and I wasn't about to let you throw that away to take pictures."

"Mother I'm sure you can see why Alec would be upset hearing this news," Eric started to say.

"You always did spoil these children and look what almost happened. Your son almost left this place to fetch coffee for some photographer. You should all be thanking me for stopping a horrible mistake!"

"Dad, can I be excused?" Alec asked quietly. He needed to leave and do it before he said something he couldn't take back. Alec didn't get angry often, but when he did it was ugly.

"Me too," Madison said as her dad nodded his head yes.

"I don't ask for permission, I'm a heathen," Sugar said, following her brother and sister outside.

Alec was in rare form as he paced the front porch like a caged tiger.

"How the hell could she do that?" he raged. "She speaks of it like it's nothing. Nothing!"

The front door opened and Eric stepped out. "Come on, you three, sit down," he said, pointing to the big porch swing.

Alec sat in the middle with both of his sisters at his side.

"I need you to forgive her and come back to breakfast," Eric said.

"Huh?" Alec said. "No way that's happening. She's not even sorry, Dad!"

Eric closed his eyes as he stood in front of his three children. "I'm asking you to. She's sick, Alec. She doesn't have much time left. She's my mother—" he said as his jaw quivered.

The three jumped out of the swing and wrapped their arms around their father.

"She told me when she got in yesterday. Remember she said she was sick at Christmas and couldn't come? That was real. She tried some experimental treatments and hoped we'd never know how bad it was."

"I'll act like it never happened," Alec promised.

"Me too," Madison added.

"I'll try," Sugar said sheepishly, bringing some much-needed humor to the conversation.

"All right, let's head back in," Eric said after he got his emotions back under control.

⁂

Alec knocked on the front door of his father's house, hoping to catch him before the garden party. Since Becca first came back to town, some things had been bothering him, and he found he had more questions than answers.

So much happened so fast back then. Finding out he had a long-lost little sister definitely threw chaos into the mix, and he never got the chance to ask his father the one question burning in his mind.

Why did he marry a woman he didn't love? Were The Lodge and the money that came with it really more important to him than love? Maybe he was afraid of losing his father's approval. Alec had no doubt in his mind that his grandfather would withhold not only the business and money from Eric, but also his love.

When his parents first divorced, it was so difficult. Both his grandparents had recently died in a car accident, and then his parents announced they were getting divorced practically before they laid the grandparents to rest. There was so much change at one time. It was hard to grasp.

Eric and Allison were so much happier divorced, and there were zero issues between them. Soon Alec realized their divorce wasn't about to disrupt their entire lives. His parents were great friends after the split and co-parented together perfectly.

If Alec had been a little older and a little wiser, he would have realized that nothing changed but a piece of paper saying the two were married. They lived in a massive house growing up, and his parents didn't share a bedroom their whole married life. An excuse of Eric's epic snoring was always used, but that's not how marriage works.

Things started clicking in place when they sat Alec and Maddie down a little over a year later and told them that Allison was a lesbian and that their "Aunt" Mary was her partner. They'd grown up with Aunt Mary, their mom's best friend from college. She worked at the hotel with Allison, and they were never apart.

Apparently, Eric knew of his wife's sexual preference right before Alec and Madison were born. The marriage was a complete sham orchestrated by their two grandfathers, and they had never loved each other that way.

Madison's horrendous behavior started around this time as the gossip mill when into full production. Alec rolled with it like he always does. He never wanted to be a problem, and this was no different.

Looking back with fresh eyes, he knew it would be different for Madison. Those girls at school were like sharks circling prey. No one would treat him that way, and he felt a little ashamed that he never took her feelings into consideration. He could have made it clear it wasn't okay to pick on Madison and they wouldn't have done it.

No, he was to wrapped up in his own little world at the time. Compared to him, his twin had it more difficult than him in every way. His grandfather never treated her like he treated Alec. He should have said something – done something.

Now that everything was semi-calm, all these things emotions and questions were popping up. Alec about turned away from the door when it opened.

"Hi, Alec." Becca's smiling face greeted him. Even with the big curlers in her hair, she was beautiful. "Come on in."

Becca was one of the nicest people Alec knew. So kind and beautiful, she made his father deliriously happy. She was a great addition to the family, but seeing his father with Becca brought many questions.

"Thanks," he said as he entered their happy little house.

Much like Sugar and Jackson's home, this house was a significant departure from growing up in the main house. However, unlike Sugar's home, drywall was installed, covering the natural wood on the walls. The beautiful wood beams that made up the high ceiling were still visible, but the addition of the drywall made it look more like a traditional home.

Decorated in blues and yellows, it was comfortable and homey, two things the house he grew up in definitely weren't. Big windows highlighting the forest behind the house showed Eric outside tending to a raised garden bed.

"Head on out back," Becca said.

Grateful when she didn't follow, Alec opened the big French door. Their patio was a lot like their house—comfortable and inviting. Chairs with oversized pillowy cushions striped blue were placed around a firepit. A barbeque and indoor kitchen were just off the patio, with a pergola roof and bar top.

"Alec," Eric said with a smile. "And before you ask, yes, you have to go to your grandmother's garden party."

"I know better than that," Alec said as he began helping his dad pull weeds from the containers. "I wanted to make sure you're okay with everything."

Eric sadly shook his head. "It's something we all have to go through. Mother thinks she has maybe a couple of weeks at best. I'm still trying to digest that. But no matter how old you are, it's hard to think about not having parents," he said honestly.

"Well, I'm here if you need anything," Alec said earnestly. Eric had always been Alec's hero. He was just the right mix of tough and tender.

"I appreciate that," Eric said. "Now, what else is on your mind?"

Alec looked up from pulling weeds and saw his father looking at him with a half-smile. Parents always knew, didn't they?

"I don't want to burden you anymore with my bullshit," Alec said.

Eric walked around the large, raised bed and put his arm around his son's shoulders. "Come on and sit down," he said, leading him back to the patio. Opening the fridge in the outdoor kitchen, he grabbed a couple of beers and handed one to Alec. "It's my job to take your burden."

Alec sat down by the firepit in one of the comfortable chairs. "Why did you marry Mom?"

"That's complicated," Eric said, looking Alec right in the eyes.

"I know it is, but it just doesn't make sense. I mean, once Mom came out, and I started hearing stories about Becca . . ." Alec took a deep breath. "Was it the money or the business that was more important than love or Becca? I've seen how happy you are with her. It doesn't make sense."

Alec registered the shocked look on Eric's face. "Alec, there are things you don't understand, don't know," he said carefully. "But neither of those reasons are why I married your mother instead of Becca. I had my reasons, and you may not want to know them."

"That's the thing, Dad," Alec said. "I may not want to know them, but I need to know them. Back then, I thought the business must be everything, that this legacy was more important than even love."

Eric closed his eyes. "Nothing could be further from the truth, Alec. I would have given up everything to be with Becca from the beginning."

"Then why didn't you?" Alec prodded.

"Alec, is this why you haven't really had a proper relationship?" Eric asked with concern. "Your photography?"

"In part, I guess," Alec said. Then, after taking a sip of his beer, he continued. "I always wanted to be just like you. If being a part of The Lodge was so vital that you'd marry someone you didn't love, why even try to find that kind of connection?"

"Oh, Alec . . ."

"And the photography, well, I suppose it's part of my decision to devote my life here." Alec sat looking at his fingernails like they were the most exciting thing on earth. Now that he was talking about it, he couldn't stop. "I couldn't devote my life to my photography, so I put it away. It hurt to think about selling it or having a show in a gallery. I told myself having a few pictures around town was enough."

LEAVING HOME   **149**

Alec got the courage to look up, and his heart broke at the devastated look on his father's face.

"My god," Eric said. "Alec, I am so sorry you've felt this way all these years."

Taking a deep breath, Eric pulled a chair up next to his son. "I've always thought I was protecting you, but I never realized I might be hurting you."

"So tell me why," Alec pleaded.

"Have you ever heard any rumors about my father, your grandfather?"

John Larsson was always a topic of conversation when he was alive, and when Alec was younger. The man ran the business with an iron fist and was known as someone you just did not mess with.

"Of course I did," Alec answered. "Everyone was either in love with the man or terrified of him."

"Did you ever hear the one about Paul Anderson's first wife?" he asked.

He probably heard that story more than any of them. Jackson's father, Paul, had a quickie marriage in his youth, and it went sour fast. There was no prenup, and she vowed to take as much of the business as she could.

Before any of it could get to court, the woman went over the side of the mountain, and after investigation, it was found her brakes had failed. The rumor around town was that John Larsson cut the brake lines, and since he had the police under his thumb, he was never charged.

"Oh yeah, the kids loved pulling out the 'your grandfather is a murderer' at school," Alec said. "I asked him about it once."

"What?" Eric asked, appearing shocked to his very

core. By his reaction Alec properly guessed that his father never did just that – ask the man if he actually did it.

"Yeah, I got tired of hearing it. So one day when I was in fifth grade, I asked him when we were fishing," Alec said. "He said it wasn't true, but he was glad people thought it because he could use it as a weapon. It was one of his many life lessons on being the King of this here empire. Even as a kid, I knew it was messed up to be happy people thought you were a murderer."

"He did weaponize it. And he aimed that weapon at me, son," Eric said. "I wasn't going to marry your mother and told him as much. I was planning on meeting Becca in California once I was done with school. Your grandfather reminded me of the incident and told me the same thing would happen to Becca or even your grandmother if I didn't comply."

"My god," Alec sputtered. "But you believed him? How could you think that of your own father?"

"He wasn't the best father growing up, Alec. He was abusive, and it took me a long time to realize how that affected me," he said. "He was bad enough that I had no qualms thinking he would murder someone before he'd let them take something from him."

Alec was utterly dumbfounded. He'd heard whispers about his grandfather, and as a child he spent as little time as possible with the man. Alec knew it sounded horrible, but things were so much better once he was gone.

"I'm so sorry," Alec said. "Then you got saddled with twins on top of it."

"No, don't you ever say that!" Eric exclaimed. "I wouldn't change a single thing in my life because if I did it would eliminate you and Madison. If anything, you all are what gave me purpose and happiness. Without you, my life wouldn't have had any joy, so don't you dare think that."

Both men stood up and embraced. "I'm so sorry you had the wrong impression for so long," Eric said as he released his son. "I hate to think you aren't doing what you want to do with your life."

"No, that's not true," Alec said. "I love it here, and nowhere else could ever be my home. I found that out when I was in college. I just needed to find my own purpose here, and you let me do that."

The father and son said their goodbyes, and even though it sounded so cliché, Alec felt like a great weight had been lifted from his shoulders as he drove away.

When would people learn that half-truths, or not talking at all led to so many unnecessary problems? His sister Sugar had the same problem with Becca, only telling her part of the story while growing up. Sometimes, when you try to protect the ones you love, you hurt them, and Alec was glad all the cards were on the table now.

☙

"Wow, so it was his grandmother the whole time?" Emery asked as she headed toward the garden party with Sugar, Jackson, and Violet.

"Yep, but we are acting like it didn't happen and that she's wonderful for Dad's sake," Sugar said.

Handing Jackson her phone the two friends posed in

front of the giant entrance to The Lodge with Violet in front. Violet's face would be blurred on the social media posts as always.

It would be intact on the Violet Jones Anderson private page, which Emery had every intention of giving Violet on her 16th birthday. Sugar was adamant that her child would not appear on anything social. As she put it Violet wasn't old enough to decide if she wanted to be an influencer. For every blurred out picture there was another one just waiting for her to grow up.

He took several pictures and handed the camera back. Emery went over each one with a critical eye and gave Jackson the thumbs up, signaling a retake wouldn't be needed. Sugar was so lucky. Jackson never complained about helping.

Jackson opened the giant lodge door and they stepped inside. The place always took Emery's breath away. Just the right amount of rustic here, just the right amount of class there—the location was perfect. She'd never toured any of the cabins that the elite rented, but she could only imagine how beautiful they were.

The truth was, Emery loved events like this. She felt like a million dollars in her soft mint green jumpsuit. It was off the shoulders and the pant legs hit just above the ankle. White, strappy heeled sandals and a white bag completed the look.

Sugar looked gorgeous in another sundress—this one had light-blue flowers that made her eyes pop. Her long blonde hair was wrapped in a braid around her head with little wisps falling out. Emery and Violet wore their hair the same way, much to Violet's delight.

"Hey, Em," Alec said with that sexy smile. Anyone else

would seem downright creepy saying her name that way, but not Alec.

"Hi, Alec." Emery just shook her head when he smiled bigger.

"Oh, you've all made it," Caitlin said.

She gave Emery a once-over and handed her glass to her. "Please be a dear and refill my water. I'm positively parched!"

"Emery doesn't work here, Grandma," Alec said while taking the glass from her.

"Why would you think she works here?" Sugar asked but Emery grabbed her hand and gave it a squeeze.

"It's fine, I'd be happy to help," Emery said with a smile.

"No need. Suzanne," Alec said to one of the wait staff. "Could you please get my grandmother another water?"

After introductions were made, Emery got as far away from Caitlin as possible. Everything was just beautiful and she was going to enjoy herself.

"God, I wish I were tall," Madison said as she found Emery on the outside wall of the veranda. "That outfit is killer."

Emery smiled. "Thanks but look at you. That dress is amazing. See, you want to be taller; I want to have curves like you. We are never happy with what we have."

"I suppose, but I'd still look like a short little corn stalk if I wore your outfit." She took a macaron for herself and another for Emery. "I don't know, though. Having a sister like Sugar, I might not be able to fit in my clothes for much longer."

"Amen, sister, I've been dealing with that my whole life," Emery said.

"He really likes you, you know," Madison said.

Emery looked around the party. "Who are we talking about?"

"My stupid brother," Madison said. "Okay, so it might not be such a trigger for my anymore if you wanted to date him."

Emery sighed. "That just isn't in the cards. He's my best friend's brother."

Madison rolled her pretty green eyes. "You both are clueless. But look, I admit he'll be a little bit of work. He has the emotional maturity of a teenager, but think of it this way: you can mold him into what you want him to be."

"You're terrible," Emery said with a smirk. "It would be a disaster if it didn't work out."

"Ah, but what if it did?" Madison said with a smile and a wink. "There's Hunter, I'll talk to you later."

Emery was just about to re-join the party when Alec took her by the hand.

"What are you doing?" Emery asked as he pulled her along to the back stairs.

"Rescuing you," he said as they raced down the stairs.

They turned around the corner of the building and he slowed down.

"Rescuing me from what? I love garden parties," she said.

"Oh, well I guess I'm rescuing me and taking you along for the ride," he said with his cheesy grin. "Come on, there's another garden this way."

It didn't take long to arrive at the beautiful garden. A grand archway filled with climbing pink clematis flowers welcomed them. Every color of pink you could imagine grew in a large circle with four benches spaced evenly around. Gray pavers made the walkway and a gorgeous water fountain graced the middle. It was made of pure white marble and had three delicate layers.

"Alec, this is beautiful," she said once she got her breath back.

"My grandpa made this for his mother," he said. "Jackson's dad said she was a wonderful person. They were not all bad, Em—the people in my family. I'm sorry my grandmother did that to you."

"Oh, Alec, I know," Emery said. "I wouldn't think that in a million years. Don't you worry about it. It wasn't a big deal."

"Well, it was a big deal to me. If I hadn't made a promise to my dad, it wouldn't have been pretty."

"She's from another time and she doesn't have long. We aren't going to change her mind or her ways in a couple of weeks. So it's best to just let her be and hopefully she'll find some peace before she goes," Emery said.

"Have you experienced things like that in the past?" Alec asked.

Oh, he was so clueless, but it wasn't his fault. He wanted to know, so she decided to tell him.

"It depends," she said. "If I leave my hair super curly, people can't decide if I'm Mexican or African American. I get followed around in stores, like I'm going to steal. It doesn't happen if I straighten my hair because then they assume I'm Italian or something like that."

"That's terrible," he said.

"People like you wanting to know is what will make it get better Alec, so thank you for asking," she said. "I was afraid of how it might be living here, but I think I've finally come to the conclusion that I'm accepted here and I don't need to be afraid."

"Why would you be afraid of that?" Alec asked. "I think people in this town might like you more than me, and that's saying something."

She faced an internal struggle about what to say next. Emery never talked about Quentin, but maybe it was time. Talking about Josh helped Sugar get over her issues with dating. Perhaps this could help her.

"There was also a problem with a guy I dated," she said.

"Really? That Todd guy?" he asked.

Emery laughed. "No, nothing exciting would ever have happened with Todd. It was my first real boyfriend. We met in college and dated until our senior year. I was sure I would marry him. His name was Quentin and he was focused, driven, and ambitious. He came from New York and his family were old money. You know the type?" she asked.

"Yeah, one of them was just very rude to you at the garden party," he joked.

"Quentin had one goal in life, and that was to be President of the United States. He briefly met my father at a school function, but never met my mother. He always went back east for holidays and sometimes I'd go with him, but he never came to my family's holidays."

She took a deep breath. "So when he finally met my mother, well, he became distant after that. I finally confronted him, and God bless him or curse him, he told me the truth. He thought I'd have more 'white' genes than dark, and after he met my mother, he feared his children could come out looking African American if he stayed with me."

Alec looked at her and opened his mouth to speak. Closed it and opened it again.

"I just . . . wow," Alec said. "What an idiot. I mean, he did know your mother was African American?"

"Oh yes, he knew but he also knew she was part Mexican. My dad is Swedish, so I think he just assumed my mom was really light skinned too. I mean, back at home, Sugar used to get darker than me in the summer."

"I'm sorry that happened to you," Alec said sincerely.

"Thank you. I appreciate that," Emery said. "I'm sure at first he thought I'd make a perfect addition to his political agenda. They could say I was all these different races without me looking like it. Once he saw my mother it his real attitude on different races came out."

"For the record, I think your mom is hot," Alec said with a wicked grin.

"You did not just say that, Alec Larsson!"

He reached up to cradle the side of her face with his hand, his index finger trailing her cheek. "She's not as beautiful as you are. I don't think I've ever seen anyone as beautiful as you."

"Alec—" she started to say but before she could say anything else, he was giving her one of those sweet, horrendously slow kisses that plagued her dreams.

It was almost over before it began, much to her disappointment.

"I know you have reservations about us," Alec said, his hand still cradling her face. "I have a well-deserved reputation, and your best friend is my sister."

"Yes but—"

"I'm not finished," he interrupted. "While my reputation may be deserved, I was never a bad guy to anyone, and I never told lies. I still don't tell lies and I like you, Em. I like you a lot."

"So much is changing and there's so much going on," Emery said.

"I know, and I'm going to give you space. Space to get your living situation straight, get the gallery going. When you know what you want, you know where I am."

She watched him walk away, her fingertips still touching her lips.

⌘

She was losing her mind. She now realized how those people spinning multiple dishes on sticks felt. Things were speeding toward different destinations, and she just wanted to get off.

The people in the second apartment were more than happy to vacate early, especially once Emery threw in her special incentive. The workers started remodeling it, and they broke the water line, causing the whole building to be without plumbing for three days.

The next fiasco happened when she was watching Violet, and she discovered she could unlock the new partial walls that were just delivered. Unfortunately, she had one of the larger ones rolling before Emery knew it and it crashed into several others, ruining them. Poor little Violet felt so bad, but Emery just told her she made it better because now she'd have them built with locks on the locks.

If that were not bad enough, August Rainer the blogger decided he'd waited long enough and was just showing up here today. Emery quickly changed into another jumpsuit, this time a red one with spaghetti straps and gold buttons. Madison did have a point, these sure came in handy.

Stepping outside, she looked up to see that at least one thing was going right. "E Cooper Gallery" in muted burgundy ran the width of the building above the large windows. It looked perfect.

"Are you Emery Cooper?" a distinguished gentleman with graying temples and expensive sunglasses asked.

"Yes, I am," she said. "You must be August. It's a pleasure to meet you. I just love your blog."

"We're going to get along just fine, aren't we?" August joked.

"I must warn you, we aren't planning on having the opening for at least a month," Emery said as she led him into the space.

"That's beautiful," he said. Alec's picture was hanging on one of the temp walls that survived Violet's demolition derby. "Will that be in the show?" He took out his camera and took a picture of the wall.

"Oh no, that's not going to be in the show. We just put it up to see how artwork would look on the wall," Emery said, kicking herself for not thinking about it.

"Okay," he said, but Emery didn't think he believed her. "Let's get to business. So how many Becca Jones originals do you think you'll feature," he asked as he held his phone, recording the conversation.

Great, she thought. *Just great.*

☙

Alec was stomping his way to the E Cooper Gallery. This supposedly influential art blogger just released his article on her blog, and his photo was the main image for the article.

He told her he didn't want to show his work. He told her over and over but she just didn't listen. Finally, the blogger talked about how she would use the gallery to showcase new artists, and that he'd gotten the in on her first new artist.

Ridiculous. Emery was going to look silly when he didn't give her any of his photographs.

His pace slowed as he neared the gallery. However, the man did say how talented the photographer was and he was excited about seeing more of his work. Alec's anger subsided with every step as he got closer and closer to the gallery.

By the time he swung open the front door, he'd made a decision.

"Alec!" Emery exclaimed as she hurried over to him. "Oh, Alec, I did not tell that man I'd be showing your work. I swear I didn't! I had it up to check one of the walls and he barged his way in here uninvited. Please believe me," she pleaded, grabbing both of his hands.

"Doesn't matter," Alec said.

"What? Why?" Emery asked. "Alec we've known each other for quite a while now. I'd like to think you know I'm not the kind of person to lie."

"It doesn't matter because if you still want to, I'm going to have you show my work in the gallery."

Emery just stood there, staring at him.

"Did you hear me, Em?" he asked.

She let go of his hands and threw her arms around his neck, pulling him in for a kiss.

And what a kiss it was.

Emery displayed none of Alec's self-control and kissed him deeply, passionately. They were both left breathless when she finally pulled away.

"I would have given you all my photographs months ago if I knew you'd do that," he said as she laughed and hugged him.

"I don't want to be afraid," Emery said seriously as she looked into his eyes. "I'm not a hook up, or someone just out for a good time. I can't take my heart being broken again."

Pulling her close he whispered, "I think you can hurt me much worse than I can hurt you. Let's just make a deal not to hurt each other."

Emery smiled and kissed his lips. "It's a deal."

ଔ

Emery looked around the busy art gallery at people drinking champaign, nibbling on pastries, and most importantly, admiring the art. Her eclectic mix of art was a hit, and people who came in hopes of snapping up one of Becca's illustrations were now snapping up all the other art.

She wore a sleek black gown. One shoulder was bare, and the other side had a slit going halfway up her thigh. Her hair was natural and with wild curls, and her makeup just a little more glamorous than usual.

It was a crisp September night, but it didn't stop the electricity in the air. People from all walks of life filled the room, dressed in their very best. Snow Valley was hopping and every motel, hotel, and bed-and-breakfast were sold out.

Tonight was the opening, but this weekend would be the auction for Becca's illustrations. A high end auction house was handling the sale of the illustrations after they were shown in the gallery.

The outer wall with the big windows displayed items not typically shown in an art gallery. Mugs, doilies, quilts, and even origami. Every single handcrafted piece was sold within a half hour of the doors opening, and the artists that produced them gained invaluable contacts.

The back displayed Alec's photography. His grandmother's portrait hung proudly in the center, and it captured everyone's attention as they walked by. Caitlin Larsson had passed shortly after her garden party, and Eric assured Alec it was okay to display his portrait.

The middle of the gallery housed Becca's illustrations. A case dead center held the actual book Becca made by hand—a book seven-year-old Sugar gave Emery when kids were being mean to her at school. It's what started everything. The handmade treasure was just on display here. It would be going to its new home at the Smithsonian once the show was over.

It was so much more to Emery than a national treasure. That handmade book changed her life, and she knew there were plenty others out there who felt the same way. She needed to say something and just hoped she had enough of that Cooper steel running through her veins from her parents to get through it without turning into a blubbering mess.

The key would be not to look at anyone she knew while she gave her speech. Misty, a newly hired gallery employee handed Emery the microphone and took Emery's glass of champaign.

"Attention, may I have your attention please," she said as she stood in front of the case displaying the handmade book.

She waited a beat while people gathered around and came back in the main room from Sugar's dinning area. Putting pocket doors between the two buildings worked out perfectly, giving the people plenty of room to either look at the art or enjoy the fine pastries and drink provided by the Snow Globe Café.

Leaning on one of those pocket doors was her best friend in the world. Her chef's coat was open and had the hint of a tiny, protruding belly. Her husband stood behind her, his hands kneading her shoulders. Her parents stood next to her, and Becca offered Emery a supportive smile.

Right in front of her were her parents and Alec. He gave her an encouraging wink and Emery took a few deep breaths, getting her emotions under control. She was a Cooper, after all.

"I just wanted to take the time and thank you all for coming to the E. Cooper opening. I'd also like to thank this wonderful town for being so open and so accepting. All of you from out of town are in for a delight. This town is truly special, and I'm overjoyed and humbled to be a part of it now."

Emery took a breath and looked at Becca for a brief moment.

"I'd also like to thank Marie Jones, or Becca as I know her, for honoring E. Copper with her work," Emery said as she gestured towards Becca.

"This book changed many lives over the year, mine included," she said as she returned her attention to the main part of the room. "You see, when I was in elementary school, I was the victim of bullying by some children who were taught my heritage was wrong. It was only a couple of children, but it was enough."

Emery noticed some nodding heads in the crowd and continued. "Then one day this new girl started school and was in my class. Her name was Sugar Jones and she seemed reserved, almost guarded around us children. It turns out she had her own story, but that's not for tonight. Tonight is for how she noticed children picking on me, and she brought this very book to school."

She offered a smile in Sugar's direction and took another cleansing breath. "I'm sure you all know what this book is about – how a caterpillar struggles so it's wing will be strong enough to fly when it leaves the pod. Becca, I'm sorry Marie Jones, broke it down to a child's level, and it resonated with me."

Emery gently tapped the glass case. "I read this book every night before I went to sleep. One night my mother, Laura Cooper, noticed I was reading something. She asked me to get my new friend's phone number so she could find out who wrote it."

Emery couldn't help but smile. "I'd like to say that's how our parents met and that was the beginning to all of this," she said as she gestured around the room.

"But it wasn't. The very next day the main bully called me a name, a very bad slur used against African Americans. He pushed me, and Sugar Jones, God bless her, popped him right in the nose, which caused blood to go everywhere."

Alec started laughing which caused several others to

laugh. She heard a few people in the crowd say things like "Good!"

Emery held her hands out to quiet the crowd. "Anyway, the school called all three of our parents in for a meeting. The bully's parents were mortified by what he'd been doing and found out an Uncle had been teaching him those things. Once he was reprimanded, the bullying stopped. Becca met my parents, a literary agent and an entertainment lawyer. The rest, as they say, is history."

"You might be wondering why I'm offering this little walk down memory lane. This book and these illustrations are too important to just be looked at as ink on paper. This character has changed lives, has given children comfort when they needed it the most, me included."

Emery smiled at the crown. "This work needs to be honored, and I'm grateful to all of you here who are doing just that. Thank you again for coming, and I hope you have a wonderful night."

The crowd began clapping as Emery nodded. She found the courage to look over at Sugar and noticed the tears streaming down her face as poor Jackson tried to calm her. She gave her a smile and felt two familiar arms come around her. "You're amazing," Alec whispered, giving her a quick kiss behind her ear. He left just as quickly as he came, giving her room to do her job.

○₹

"I think it's going well," Laura Cooper said to her daughter. "You have an excellent mix of people here. After this they may need to open another hotel in the area. The secret's out —Snow Valley is where it's at."

Emery thanked her as she returned to Becca, ever the mother hen with her favorite client. She looked over and caught Alec's eye. He mouthed "help me" and she couldn't help but smile as a forty-year-old patron of the gallery ran her hand along his arm before deciding to save him.

"Sweetheart, there you are," he said as he pulled Emery close to his body. "This is my girlfriend, Emery. Emery, do you know Tonya?"

The rest of the night went perfect. With the pocket doors open, they had double the bathrooms and a good space for socializing. A curtain was placed in front of the bakery case and cash register, effectively hiding that a bakery existed. She rented pub-style tables where people could stand and talk but have a place for their drinks.

Becca generously was giving the money from one of the illustrations to fund the new artist residency, enabling Emery to do so much more with the upcoming program.

The remodeling of the artist in residence area was almost complete. The expanded electric for the kilns and potter's wheel were taking a little longer, and they might not be able to start the residency until January. It was disappointing but they were still moving forward.

"Chief Barker!" Emery said when she saw the policeman. "I'm so glad you could make it. I wanted to let you know that I love your daughter's art and if she's interested the first residency, it's hers!"

Emery already talked to Angelica, and while she sounded happy for the opportunity, she couldn't say the woman sounded excited. She asked for a couple of weeks to think about it, and Emery was delighted to oblige.

"Thank you, Emery, that is so generous," the Chief said. "It's hard getting that girl out of New York, but maybe this will do it. I really appreciate this."

Emery smiled and made her way to the kitchen. Sugar hadn't made an appearance since Emery's speech, and she found her in full-fledged head chef mode as she put her staff through the paces.

This was Sugar's element. Dressing up and schmoozing would never be for her but feeding those that did was right up her alley. Both Becca and Emery tried to convince her to be just a guest for the evening, but she would have none of that. Sugar insisted the night was too important to have someone muck up the food.

"That last batch of tarts looked a little blonde, people," she said.

Emery backed out, knowing better than to interrupt Sugar when she was in her element. She felt two strong arms circle her waist.

"Do you think Poppy is okay up there?" Alec asked. Alec and Poppy had moved into Emery's new apartment once it was remodeled. Just as she suspected Poppy wanted to be with Alec, no matter where he lived.

"She's fine," Emery said.

"I'm just trying to be a good cat dad," he said. "Maybe I can get one of those sweatshirts that have pouches for the cat. Have you seen those?"

"OMG, no way," Emery said as she walked back to the party.

"I can get you one too! We can get matching ones! And

another cat!" Alec said. "Don't you just love exclamation point days?"

Emery nodded her head yes and smiled at her boyfriend. She had a feeling that most days from now on would be exclamation point days.

From the Author

I cannot begin to thank each one of you who have read The Snow Globe Café series! It was a long road getting these out to you, and the big gap between the second and third book was due to an illness. Thank you for hanging in there with me. I really wanted to explain to you all because so many were excited for this one to come out!

So what's next with the series? I thought long and hard about whether I should start a new series in a new town, or if I should continue with this one.

Truth of the matter is I love these characters and I love this little town. I love the square and The Lodge and the Larsson's and the Olsson's. I want to keep up with Violet and her new twin brothers.

I've decided to carry on with The Snow Globe Café series. The upcoming books will of course have our favorite characters, but the main characters will be new, or previously minor characters.

I am very excited about some of the characters I plan to bring to you. Next up will be the story of Angelica, a gentle artist who lost her mother mid puberty. Partially estranged from her father and brother, taking the residency offered by Emery seems a good way to be close again.

Things are going to get real messy when she catches Matt's eye. Her stepsister Gina has never really cared for her, and when Matt becomes attracted to Angelica, the drama will be in full swing!

After that I plan on writing about Holly, the owner of the local flower shop. Bullied horribly as a teenager she needs to come to terms with it and move on. Her husband left her, leaving her to raise their son on her own. Can she ever open her heart to another again?

Finally, there is Lexis. I really think she is going to be the most fun I'll have writing a character. With two train wreck B List famous parents Lexis has chosen the wholesome route. She puts that in jeopardy with the slip of a few words, and she heads to Snow Valley to clean up her image.

With my health on the mend, I plan on bringing these books to you as soon as possible! Be sure to sign up for updates over at my website:

http://www.kellyjcalton.com

Follow my blog there for all updates on these upcoming books!

You can also follow me on Amazon here:

https://www.amazon.com/Kelly-J.-Calton/e/B07T315KHL

They are pretty decent at letting you know when new books come out by the authors you follow.

Thank you again from the bottom of my heart. You all are a part of my dream, and I appreciate how you have all stood by me while I was sick. It truly means the world to me!

Love,
Kelly J Calton

Made in the USA
Las Vegas, NV
25 September 2021